The Road to Moresco

Mark Jamilkowski

TREATY OAK PUBLISHERS

PUBLISHER'S NOTE

This is a work of fiction based on the author's research in historical records, family albums, private correspondence, and other similar resources.

Printed and published in the United States of America

TREATY OAK PUBLISHERS

ISBN-978-1-959127-10-9

DEDICATION

For strong, resilient, and powerful women,
especially those who have graced my life.

TABLE OF CONTENTS

T his is a story about people, places and times, but mostly a story about family and the dynamics which influence actions and reactions. We are about to take a journey that explores the unfolding of over 150 years of world history and the impact it had on the formation of a family.

Like drips of water from snow melting on a mountain top, each event in turn becomes a drip collecting with the next to form a brook, then a stream, then a river, joining with the rainwater. The journey down the mountain side runs over rough earth, a wild, twisted and turbulent journey at times. Quieting across the plateaus and plains, it turns into a gentle babble, cooing and serene. The banks of the river widen or narrow in accordance with the complexity of the family as well as the community.

A singular moment—the boulder mid-stream that must be gone around or over—affects generations yet to come downstream. We will explore how the components of history, the influence of culture and politics and the ebb and flow of other people give shape and composition to this family.

Our journey begins in mid- and late-century 1800s Sicily and Turin. But to understand the mid-1800s, we need to learn a bit more about what formed those societies beforehand. Perhaps then it will be best to start our journey with a little context. I do not think we need a deep history lesson. Rather, I will borrow a technique I used during my son's childhood.

When my son was a small child, I read bedtime stories to him. We chose from many books, since he enjoyed them all. Some nights we laughed about the adventures of an escaped gorilla and the mysterious black cat that went everywhere the gorilla went (but you had to search to find him). Or shared in moments of subtle wisdom and philosophy with our dear, dear friend and his friends by extension, so as to not leave out anyone – oh bother – we've done it again, Pooh. The fairy tales by the Brothers Grimm, specifically Rapunzel, became our favorite. Now you may remember the story Rapunzel, but I beg your forgiveness for a quick detour and overview to explain its relevance to our tale of the road to Moresco.

* * *

In Rapunzel, we meet a girl isolated in a tower by a witch, a wicked crone who treasures her and wants to possess her all for herself. A prince who finds the tower courts the girl. Her singing mesmerizes him. The girl's hair is long enough to provide the prince an opportunity to meet her. The witch discovers the betrayal.

The second part of the story is darker, resulting a thorn blinding the prince, while the spiteful, revengeful witch casts the girl out to a remote village where the blind prince will never be able to find her. But after an exhaustive search, he does stumble upon her village. She holds him in her lap, crying at his disfigurement. Her tear touches his face, his eyes are healed and they return to the kingdom together.

It is a complex tale with many subtexts as well as morals. And the full reading to a small child looking for adventure while half asleep meant attempting to complete the story over two or three nights. Soon, I came to summarize this story as "Once upon a time, there was a witch, a girl, a tower, a prince, a song and so much hair. A thorn, then darkness, then a tear, then gladness. Happy ever after, the end."

Thirty seconds, content plus context achieved and bedtime accomplished. Silly and satisfied, my son fell asleep, clutching Charlie the alligator, his protector.

And so, we must begin with the context of the road to Moresco in a similar matter, covering two thousand years of world history in a few sentences.

* * *

Once upon a time, a group of sailors fleeing Greece landed on the shores of the Mediterranean Sea, along the Tiber River. There they founded a city which came to be known as Rome. From there a juggernaut arose, a political and military power overseen by Augustus Caesar that dominated the tribal powers across most of what we now call Europe.

At its zenith, its control extended over not just Italy

and the regions around the Alps but also Britannia (England), Germania (western and southern modern-day Germany), Gallia (France), Hispania (Spain and Portugal), parts of Northern Africa (the coasts of Libya and Egypt, for example), continuing all along the shores of the Mediterranean to include Arabia, Palestine and Syria (the area known as the Levant). It took in the territories we now know as Turkey, as well Bulgaria and Romania that border the Black Sea. It encompassed the region known as Illyrium (which today includes Croatia, Bosnia, Serbia, Hungary, Slovenia and Austria) as well as Greece. It also stretched to the north to Noricum (Austria).

A collection of emperors, along with a vast network of appointed officials, ruled over this sweeping empire. The economies of this expanse, which supported its administrative and military weight, collapsed around the year 476, resulting in the formation of multiple regional and independent political entities.

A few hundred years later, Charlemagne led his troops out of Germania, sweeping west and south, once again putting a large part of Europe under one ruler. The newly combined areas were unstable and splintered once again after multiple civil wars. A few hundred years after that, in 1272, two monarchies were formed by marriages as well as acquisitions – The Bourbons and the Habsburgs.

The Bourbons were a bloodline started with the marriage of the youngest son of the King of France, King Louis IX, to the heiress of the Lordship of

Bourbon, an area of prominence in France. Some genealogical connection to the Bourbons remained in control of France and later Spain, for centuries. Branches of this family dynasty at one point also held thrones in Naples, Sicily and Parma. Bourbon bloodlines are still represented in the monarchies of Spain and Luxemburg to this day.

The Habsburg dynasty takes its name from a castle named 'Habsburg' by the family who lived there, the Radbots. Around year 1200, one of the Radbot family descendants decided to call himself the Duke of Habsburg. So it began.

Through various military victories in Bohemia (the area later considered Czechoslovakia, now the Czech Republic and Slovakia) and Austria plus many inter-family marriages, the Habsburg family tree includes emperors over Austria, Hungary, the Austria-Hungary Empire, Croatia, Portugal, part of Italy. Starting around 1450, they also enjoyed almost three hundred years of being named emperors of the Holy Roman Empire.

(N.B. Many argue this was not an empire at all but an attempt to restore prior glories of the original Roman Empire. Some also argue the name reflected political and influence-based aspirations of the Vatican during that time period).

By 1700, the fighting among different religious groups, such as the Protestants, Calvinists and Catholics, weakened the military power of the Habsburgs. Their hold declined further as a result of battles with the French on the Western edge of their empire and the Ottomans (Turks) on the Eastern border. By 1800, after unsuccessful wars against France and Napoleon, the Habsburg dynasty shrunk to only a few smaller kingdoms.

The Bourbon and Habsburg bloodlines are still counted among the rulers of many of the European empires well into the 20th century. These separate ruling monarchies kept Italy, as we know it today, divided among several different ruling interests.

In the first half of the nineteenth century, the Italians were one of the largest populations under a Habsburg monarchy. This included the provinces of Lombardy and Venetia, with the cities of Milan and Venice. The Kingdom of the Two Sicilies ruled southern Italy from Naples to Palermo.

In the early 1800s, an Italian activist, Giuseppe Mazzini, established himself as a vocal proponent for a unified Italy. His audacity and passion challenged the millennia-long bifurcation of the country since the fall of the Roman Empire. He threatened to destabilize the control current monarchies wielded. He was exiled and imprisoned, but he never relented in his pursuit of a socially conscious democracy and a unified republic. Mazzini's public arguments with and disdain for Karl Marx and Marxism also shaped his thoughts and vision for a unified Italy.

With his friend and collaborator, Giuseppe Garibaldi, Mazzini proved to be resolute and persistent. Success with the initial unification of

Italy was achieved in the mid-1800s.

Just as critical to our story, however, is that success also planted an important seed for how the people across these lands came to think of themselves. The rise of a nationalist movement at the turn of the 20th century influenced Italian leadership and the country's role in World War I, as well as World War II. Benito Mussolini rose to power by harnessing the nationalistic passion of the people.

These are the drips of water that form our landscape, shaping generations of decisions and actions. The impact of the river on our characters continues to this very day.

The stage is set. Let us begin for our travel along the Road to Moresco, a journey where a boy meets a girl, who becomes a woman and a mother, which begins another journey altogether.

Europe in 1815

https://upload.wikimedia.org/wikipedia/commons/a/ac/Europe_1815_map_en.png and access date was 5/16/22

Italy in 1815

https://rsc.byu.edu/mormons-piazza/great-basin-kingdom-king-
dom-sardinia-1849-51 and the footnote on that page says "Re-
printed form George Homes, ed., *The Oxford History of Italy
(New York*: Oxford University Press, 1997), 182"

CHAPTER 1

Marcello il Padre e Messina, Vos Benedicimus

On December 27, 1910, Francesca and Giuseppe Carnabuci headed home from the evening's religious festivities. They meandered along the cobblestone streets of Messina, Sicily, that cut into the hillside and foothills of Mt. Etna. Their church had been decorated with all the ornamentation in celebration of Christmas. Parties and events had taken place all that week, including parades and processions through the piazza they crossed that night on their way.

The stone church clock tower that lined the edge of the piazza rang out. The lingering notes of choirs and concerts floated in the night air like petal wisps cast from a blooming chestnut tree and carried aloft in the evening ocean breeze.

Francesca turned to Guiseppe and squeezed his hand. "I'm really excited for this year's New Year. The planning committee has come up with some very special performances to commemorate January 1 and our celebration of Mary."

"I'm glad the committee elected you to be the chair this year," said Guiseppe. "It's a role you carry with pride and honor."

"We even overcame Josephine's doubts, despite all her efforts to subdue the festival."

"Josephine's insistence that Mary, Mother of God, did not write a letter to the people of Messina is tiresome," Giuseppe snorted. "The inscription in the harbor wall comes directly from her letter – why else would 'Vos et ipsam civitatem benedicimus' be carved into the wall?"

"I know she is difficult. Josephine is an eternal skeptic who always insists the letter and the inscription that means 'We bless you and your city' are just too obvious a ploy by the ruling classes of Messina to make their city appear favored over Palermo." Francesca sighed. "She was born in Palermo, so we really cannot expect her to believe otherwise."

Guiseppe smiled into the moonlit eyes of Francesca. She impressed him with her capacity for compassion and understanding. Her patience just made her even more beautiful to him, even radiant in moonlight that evening.

"I appreciate your sweet temper, love. Especially because her husband is my boss," said Guiseppe with a chuckle. He laughed at the unnecessary emphasis. His wife was wise, even as she held fast to her convictions, and completely capable to navigate any political sensitivities. He squeezed Francesca's hand in return.

The moon lit their way, giving the city a vibrancy even in the subdued shadows of the winter evening. The absence of color invited their minds to recall the daytime explosion of multi-colored homes, reflecting the sun in burnt-umber, orange, white-wash, red and stone hues.

After rounding the corner, Giuseppe and Francesca arrived home. They shared a villa with another couple Guiseppe knew from childhood. Although a bit more expensive than others closer to the warehouse district down the hill nearer the port, Giuseppe loved this house. He treasured being close to his neighborhood, along with the people and memories he cherished since his father passed away a few years prior.

Once he unlocked the door, they walked up the stairs. "I'm going to sleep well tonight," he said.

After they undressed and bathed, they changed into their night shirts, climbed into bed, and soon fell asleep.

The sound of shattering plates and the bookshelf crashing to the floor jolted Guiseppe and Francesca from their dreams. As books scattered across the bedroom floor, Francesca screamed in terror.

Guiseppe jumped up and grabbed their coats and shoes. "Come! Quick!" He seized her hand, heading for the stairway.

Another shockwave rumbled, knocking them off their feet. Francesca grasped for Guiseppe, catching his night shirt to prevent him from careening down the stairs. The walls cracked, the earth moaned, the roof tiles exploded around them. They reached the bottom of the stairs just as at 5:20 a.m. on the morning of December 28th a massive earthquake rocked the seabed under the Strait of Messina, a narrow waterway between Sicily and lower mainland Italy, where the waters of the Ionian and Tyrrhenian Seas meet.

They watched as their home shifted and crumbled, then both of them fell to the cold cobblestone curb.

The crisp morning air and faint light at daybreak kept their senses alert among the nearby din of other people screaming, crying, or shouting. The dust rose as did the cries for help as more buildings collapsed or were damaged. When Guiseppe stood, he could now see the port, since the buildings that obstructed line of sight were gone. His skin tingling, the hair stood on the back of his neck. The port did not appear to have any water in it. Moored ships lay on their side or had settled into the mud.

"Run, Francesca! Holy Mother of God! Run!" he shouted and once again grabbed Francesca's hand.

"Ow! My ankle," she screamed as she stumbled against him.

He picked her up and raced toward the hill, gathering a crowd, a reverse tide of people, all wild and wide-eyed. Halfway up, he stopped to catch his breath.

Amid frantic shouts to anyone along the way,

everyone ran away from the harbor, farther up the steep slopes of Mt. Etna. Turning to look over his shoulder, Guiseppe gasped as the roiled waters of the Strait rose over 100 feet and came crashing down on the shores of eastern Sicily, devastating Messina as far as he could see.

He scooped Francesca into his arms once more. "We have to keep going higher or we will die!"

Many days later Guiseppe learned how the earthquake plus the tsunami had damaged or destroyed almost ninety percent of the buildings in Messina. Over 100,000 people perished as it wiped out several coastal towns. The massive columns and pillars of the port businesses, seats of government and palaces, with their red clay tile scalloped roofs lining the shore, were either crushed or completely gone. The merchant ships that had arrived from and sailed to Naples or Syracuse were shattered like matchsticks.

"I've worked for various merchant families throughout the years," he told Francesca later. "I worry about what happened to them." He sighed. "I also wonder if I will find work there ever again."

Over the next few weeks, survivors were forced to decide whether to rebuild, or move on. Most settled into make-shift shantytowns just outside of Messina, while some departed, becoming refugees in towns less affected.

Giuseppe chose Santa Teresa di Riva, a small town just south from Messina along the coast of Sicily, about half-way between Messina and Taormina, nestled up against the mountains and the foothills of Mt Etna.

"You will like the birds in this place," he told Francesca their first morning after they arrived. "So many different kinds."

"Like what?" She sat down across from him at the only table in the small kitchen and rested her foot on his knee.

"Warblers, fire crests, and flycatchers are pretty common. Also, black francolin and red-legged partridges strut and put on quite a show." He gave her ankle a gentle massage.

"We'll enjoy that, won't we?"

"And you can hear the screech of falcons mixed with the spotted woodpeckers, like a band of musicians."

Francesca closed her eyes as she inhaled. "I smell herbs blended with the salt of the sea spray."

"Oh, yes," Giuseppe said, "when your ankle is better, you can buy saffron, basil, fennel and capers at the market."

"I'm glad you told me," she said as she opened her eyes, smiling at him. "Now I have something to tell you."

Giuseppe raised his eyebrows and waited.

"I'm pregnant."

***

Marcello Carnabuci laughed a lot as a baby, gurgling with glee whenever his parents cooed or dangled his rattle. His parents were kind and gentle, they always seem to have just enough. Just enough food, just enough clothes, just warm enough during chilled winter nights, just enough space for their small family.

The earthquake had damaged the apartment they lived in, however it never quite got repaired. The windows were drafty, the plaster walls cracked in various places. The stairwell tilted. On each floor, tenants shared a bath at the end of the hall. Each apartment provided an ice box, a stove, plus a sink.

On Tuesdays, Thursdays and Saturdays, Francesca took Marcello to the market to purchase staples. By the age of four, Marcello's high spirit and unbridled energy bubbled over as he ran ahead into the market, hiding from his mother in between the various stalls, though he made sure to avoid anywhere near the fresh fish. Then, at the right moment, he popped out, trying to surprise Francesca.

The market bustled with adventuresome smells and delights, chili peppers, spices and cakes. "Momma, I love the almond cakes!" he called out over the shouts of the sellers trying to attract customers as the throng passed by.

Marcello watched what his mother looked at with great interest. "Do you need some of this Momma?" Marcello said, holding up a jar of *u strattu*. When his mother bought the *u strattu*, the tomato paste she used to thicken her sauces and stews, dinner was going to be special.

"We haven't eaten octopus in a while," he said. "It's one of my favorite meals, so please get some black and green olives, also more tomatoes."

"Marcello, what do you want me to do, buy everything in the market? The shrimp are fresh today, see?" Francesca smiled when his face lit up, glad of his enthusiasm for her cooking.

Not that Giuseppe ever complained, she thought.

Marcello's excitement made it extra special. His infectious energy motivated her to want to do more for him. How he inspired her! She often wondered if his charisma and lively spirit would affect others in his life in a similar manner.

Francesca saw how Marcello's mouth watered at the mere thoughts of what dinner could be. "I have everything I need. Let's go home now."

Marcello took this cue to rush ahead, his boundless impatience and energy taking control of his body.

They returned from market laughing, replaying the moments Marcello had surprised his mother, or joking about how the fish watched him from their bed of ice. Marcello skipped along or ran ahead to chase the pigeons and buttercup chickens in the street or throw pebbles at the jackdaws hiding in the crevices and cornices of the buildings along their route home.

On one occasion, his pebble missed its mark, hitting instead the woman watering her flowers that cascaded below her window. He never did get a full explanation from his mother as to what that woman shouted at them.

Marcello loved playing with Pedro, the family's pet green parakeet. Pedro bobbed as he twittered, excited when Marcello and his mother came home from the market. Marcello held him and gave Pedro treats to calm him when the marlins that nested in the eaves squawked and chattered during their dusk feeding.

During rainy days, Marcello played in the puddles, floating sticks in the rivulets formed as the water wended its way along the cobblestones and street tiles, then followed the rippling waters and bumping sticks on their journey. He imagined sailing the ship through raging waters, commanding his men to weather the storm, guiding them safely through the dangerous and rocky shores.

On the more frequent sun-soaked, warmer days, the family strolled down the hill to the shore. Marcello played in the waves, ran along the pebbled beach, or chased the terns or sandpipers. When not holding his son in the waves or playing in the sand with Marcello, his father rested and watched the elegant herons, egrets and glossy ibis hunt for sardines and small crustaceans.

Marcello's eyes were a deep-set blue, his complexion a slight olive tone, and his hair almost black. As he got older, Marcello grew thin and tall for his age, a bit lanky. Athletics did not come by nature to him, though he liked to climb chestnut or pine trees and play soccer with his friends.

Sometimes Marcello's father joined in, coaching them. "Stop crowding the ball." "Play your position." "No, stop, look - you are kicking each other and not the ball!" Giuseppe tried to maintain a calm patience against their collective instinct to chase the ball.

Giuseppe also took every opportunity to teach them about the various types of birds they saw. Marcello's father admired the special beauty of the European bee-eater. He called it an 'artist's rendering' of a bird, with a deft mix of auburn reds, umber, turquoise blues, pale yellows and hints of black. "The bee-eater combines rarity, graceful flight and skillful plumage. All that sets this one apart, in my eyes."

Marcello appreciated his father's sense of beauty and grace, but he drew inspiration from the brute power and majesty of the Lanner falcon with its white-spotted, broad muscular chest.

As the flocks of sparrows swirled into the dusk sky, the sun descended beyond Etna and the Tyrrhenian Sea, the red and purple night hues signaling the time to go home. His mother prepared the meal, while his father read a story to him as he lay down.

Refugees like his parents had trouble finding work. The rebuilding of Messina's economy dragged at a very slow pace.

One day, Giuseppe came home excited. "Some business returned to the port. They offered me a post on a freighter that ships goods between Sicily and Naples."

"Won't you be gone for long periods of time?" Marcello said, looking up at his father.

Giuseppe sighed at his son's innocence and naivete.

"Marcello, you have to understand," Francesca said. "Your father's pay provides for the family. Plus, it's a source of pride and honor for him, even if it means being away from us for long periods of time."

"We all have to do our part," Giuseppe said. "Your mother helps some of our neighbors by cooking extra meals and helping them with laundry. So, you see we all have a job to do. We commit ourselves to hard work and some sacrifice because we are a family. You, too, someday, will be ready to accept this responsibility."

Frowning, Marcello folded his arms across his chest.

Supplies ran short with greater frequency. Black markets filled the gaps, creating an opportunity for families with the means and organization to form militia-like groups. They regulated prices and controlled distribution of supplies. Santa Teresa di Riva was not immune to this encroaching post-destruction, opportunity-driven crime wave.

On Marcello's 6th birthday, in 1917, Italy entered World War I, declaring war against the Austria-Hungarian Empire. Unbeknownst to young Marcello, a thirst swelled for a stronger national identity in other parts of Italy, a movement that escaped the attention of Sicily. This zealous nationalist move-ment originated in Italian philosophy and political ideology going back over 100 years.

"This guy, Gabriele D'Annunzio, he's dangerous because of what he says and how he stirs up this nationalist discontent," Giuseppe said to one of his friends one night over an espresso on the piazza as they watched the remainder of the day slip away over the Tyrrhenian Sea and the foothills of Mt. Etna. "Ever since he made that speech a few years ago in 1915, this guy, a poet and playwright, now became suddenly some sort of politico?" Giuseppe pounded his fist on the table.

"I remember that speech, Giuseppe. The reports of it were both inspiring and terrifying. He manipulated that large crowd in Rome, his speech described as musical, rhythmic and hypnotic. His cadence reported as being irresistible," said Salvatore. "I agree he is dangerous, though. With an influence that strong on a crowd of that size, what will happen when he is no longer trying to drive policy and encourage the unification of all of Italy? I'm also not sure I agree with his war rhetoric to fight the Austrians and free the Dalmatian states."

"You see, Salvatore, that's the issue. You have daughters. I worry for my son. This guy wants people to 'do their duty' for the country, while he talks of war to regain Venice, Trieste, and Fiume as pure Italian city-states. Now it's our sons who get thrown into that zeal."

Giuseppe furrowed his brow. "You studied Mazzini in school, right? 'On the Duties of Man' and all that. We are a long way from 1858 and fighting the Bourbons or Hapsburgs." His face flushed crimson red. "We are a long way from motivating tribes to think of the nation of Italy as God's providence, to inspire a duty among disparate fiefdoms to perform for the whole, to support the nation as well as each other, before exercising individual rights."

"I recall Mazzini," Salvatore said, "and how he also emphasized inspirational phrasing over the ideas because he wanted to appeal to the masses. He wanted to get past economic and educational differences. As for D'Annunzio, I understand." Salvatore sighed. "The crowds chanted something like 'We are ready to join, we are ready to die, Italy has called' in reply to D'Annunzio's speech."

Salvatore regarded Giuseppe with a brotherly gaze. "We will watch it carefully, yes?"

"Yes," Giuseppe said with a slight shake of his head, "we must."

Despite Giuseppe's best efforts to dissuade his son, the stories of D'Annunzio's acts of heroism enthralled Marcello. There seemed to be almost daily recounting of his actions in the newspaper founded by Benito Mussolini in 1914, *Il Popolo d'Italia.*

"When I grow up, I want to be just like D'Annunzio," he said one morning over breakfast.

Wincing, Giuseppe glanced at Francesca and looked away when she bit her lip.

Giuseppe's concerns had valid foundation. That year, the military communication to Italian soldiers used Mazzini's principles of duty and country to inspire soldiers, framing their fighting as part of the "religion of duty". These inspirational phrases had a deep influence on one soldier in particular, Benito Mussolini. No one, least of all Marcello, foresaw what ripple effect that would have on their lives and also their deaths.

In 1918, Austrian airmen bombed ships heading into Naples as part of an embargo on the city. They dropped bombs on the merchant ship Giuseppe worked on, sinking it as it sailed from Messina to Naples. All aboard the ship were killed.

Marcello retreated into his heroic fantasies to distract himself from his father's permanent absence and to block out his mother's anguished crying.

As D'Annunzio flew multiple bombing missions over Trieste and Vienna, Marcello romanticized and replayed them with his makeshift stick planes as he imagined D'Annunzio avenged his father's death by bombing the enemy as they destroyed his father's ship.

While Marcello re-enacted the Vienna campaign almost daily, he did not realize that, in fact, D'Annunzio had risked a round-trip flight to Vienna from Venice to drop pamphlets, not bombs. The leaflets were meant to inspire the Viennese to revolt against their leaders, using poetry to remind them that the war now encroached on their doorsteps as well. The mission earned D'Annunzio the Croix de Guerre medal from the French government.

In September 1919, Marcello read about D'Annunzio's most famous feat, marching a small troop of elite Italian soldiers out of Venice to capture the city of Fiume (currently called Rijeka, Croatia). France and England promised Fiume, a mostly Italian-speaking city along the Dalmatian Coast, to Italy as inducement to enter the war in the first place. However, the Treaty of Versailles drew the borders of a new country, Yugoslavia, to include Fiume. Italian regular troops, deployed to protect Fiume with orders to stop D'Annunzio, were waiting for him as he approached the city. The newspapers reported how D'Annunzio, seeing the troops, delivered a speech that inspired the soldiers to join him instead of turning him away. He entered the city uncontested, the entire parade chanting "Viva l'Italia."

Marcello called to Francesca, "Mom, did you see what he did? He just walked right in! Isn't that amazing? Who else could do that?"

Francesca wiped her palms on the kitchen dish towel in silence, wringing her hands a little harder, listening to the voice of Giuseppe whisper in her ear. "It is very exciting to see that happen, but he should be obeying the international law as well as the peace treaty, don't you think, pichon?"

Marcello laughed. This year he stood as tall as his mother, but she still called him 'little one'.

"Mom, this is more than just disobeying. The newspapers bemoaned the insult to Italy, the disrespect by these other countries. He is doing the right thing. I'm not the only one, you know," he said as he rustled the newspaper, "because the papers also say thousands of other people are going to Fiume to be part of the energy and newness and excitement D'Annunzio has created."

"I've read the stories, too, Marcello," Francesca said, nodding, "and while D'Annunzio has some gripping ideas about what freedoms, what rights people should have, it is not that easy on a larger national kind of scale. Someday in school, I have no doubt you will debate the merits of his constitution for Fiume. From what I have read, the Carta del Carnaro has some interesting notions for how a democracy can function in a socialist government."

"I don't know, Mom, it just feels like things need to change. Reading about what he is doing in Fiume makes me feel proud to be Italian. Like I am part of something bigger that just our little town or just in Sicily. It all seems real somehow." Marcello paused and then added, "Plus, the Allied insistence about the terms of the Treaty of Versailles is just them being bullies. They cannot admit they're making a mistake."

"I can see you are excited by the stories, but be aware, Marcello," Francesca said in a firm tone, "because if this nationalism is achieved through revolution, then the energy and inspiration you hear about, what you feel, will not lead to a new world order, with equality and freedom, or emphasis on music, arts and beauty. Saying everything is acceptable in the name of national identity, I fear, will result in abuse from a political reign of power and terror."

As Francesca sat down at the kitchen table, her shoulders sagged. She prayed to herself, This is exhausting, Giuseppe, please guide me. Francesca sighed.

Francesca hoped the signing of the treaty, the ousting of D'Annunzio from Fiume, along with his unceremonious exit and retirement to Lake Garda, would quell Marcello's fascination with the whole matter. "I object to the school curriculum including studies of D'Annunzio's poems and his other literature," she told the administration.

It seemed, though, that every day's lesson made Francesca lose just a little bit more sleep and get a few more gray hairs.

"Mom!" Marcello called, bounding through the door, "Did you know Cardinal Fabrizio Ruffo rallied Calabria troops in 1799 to defend against a French invasion?" Marcello dropped his books on the table. "It's the same message, don't you see? His words were different – 'defend the honor of religion, King, fatherland and family' – but it's the same!"

Francesca felt the gray spreading.

The following school term, Marcello completed a study of Giuseppe Garibaldi. The unlikely success of the mission impressed Marcello. "Garibaldi led a volunteer army called 'red shirts' against the

Bourbons, French and Normans to unify all of Italy in 1860. The odds he could succeed against such well financed and trained troops is staggering."

Francesca nodded. "Yes, Marcello, the Risorgimento that created 'Italy' as a country was an important time for us all." She paused to choose her words with care. "You will see, in your studies of Mazzini, how during that time period, people were very focused on having a nation led by the people for the people, not external monarchs, the Pope, or other financial or social elites." Francesca tilted her head to one side. "You should also recall how your father argued that those ideas were for a different time. Now is different. Always remember this, Marcello."

Marcello mumbled something under his breath, a partial acknowledgment of something spoken in his presence without any confirmation it had landed anywhere near his brain.

For his twelfth birthday, Marcello's mother once again pulled together one of his favorite meals. Something felt different that year. The empty chair at the table perhaps seen for the first time. Perhaps triggered by memories of his father, who also liked the simple yet delicious grilled shrimp and spaghetti olio e pepe.

Marcello sat looking out the window, Pedro the parakeet on his shoulder, struggling to remember some of the conversations with his father. "I'm trying to name which bird makes that warble coming in through the open window."

The moment felt like a weight of stone on his chest, crushing him, pushing air out of his lungs, suffocating him. The absence created a vacuum with palpable intensity. "I miss my father," he whispered.

On Saturday, April 17, 1926, Francesca called out to Marcello, "I have to go to the market. There have been worse and worse shortages every year since that tsunami and the war... that Spanish Flu. Stay here – I should be back soon."

"Mom, hasn't the market been getting violent? I heard people calling those who run the market 'Mafia' and they get rough when people complain whenever things are not available."

Francesca had experienced a couple of situations where things distributed under Mafia supervision were exhausted before everyone in line could be satisfied. They kept order, even though some people required violence to hear.

"I'll be careful," she said. "I know my way around the hotheads." She kissed Marcello on the forehead. "Ciao, pichon."

For almost an hour Francesca waited in line. She stood on tiptoe at what sounded like shouts up ahead. She could not tell what going on, but the crowd grew louder. Several quick explosions boomed, as gunshots rang out to disperse the rioters. People bolted in several directions, uncertain where the danger came from or where safety waited. Francesca turned to run, but the man in front of her knocked into her. They fell together. She covered her head to avoid being kicked in the stampede. She stood up as soon as she could, bruised and disoriented. She scurried without having any sense of where she should go.

The gunshots rang out again, but now they fired into the crowd to stop protestors still pushing forward. Francesca felt the burning sear as the hot metal burrowed into her back and exploded in her lung. She collapsed, wheezing, "Pichon!"

Marcello had regarded his father's death as being his duty to his country, to his nation, but his mother's death seemed senseless to him. "That bullet may have taken my mother's life," he told a friend, "but it has also created new sense of determination in me to grow up, to work, to get away, to be part of the future of Italy, to honor the sacrifices my parents made, even at the expense of my own life."

Mussolini became dictator of Italy. He prioritized breaking the economic stranglehold of the Mafia and appointed Cesare Mori to lead the effort. Mori used aggressive tactics to capture over 11,000 people affiliated with Mafia activities across Sicily. Mussolini's proactive, action-oriented government and anti-Mafia stance excited Marcello. Allied politically and philosophically with Mori and Mussolini, Marcello redoubled his nationalist and fascist beliefs, ideals that were the very antithesis of the opportunistic, abusive tactics of the Mafia.

At the age of sixteen, Marcello, having no remaining family or ties to Santa Teresa di Riva,

Messina, or Taormina, left Sicily for work and to attend university in Venice. "Venice is a Renaissance city. I can create a fresh start in this vibrant, forward-thinking culture. I need to unshackle myself from the limited prospects in Sicily... its painful memories."

Venice reverberated with excitement, an urgency of renewal stemming from its liberation from the Austrian empire. He felt free, free to follow his dream of becoming an actor and poet like D'Annunzio. "I'll make a difference to Italy, my country."

Once in Venice, Marcello joined the Opera Nazionale Balilla (ONB), the National Youth Organization, started in 1926 to organize and teach the youth about Fascist ideology. Marcello and the other older boys (aged fourteen-eighteen) were called *Avanguardisti*. Each group included a Vatican-appointed chaplain who led the religious worship portion of the training, but Marcello mistrusted the chaplain.

"I hear rumors regarding the priest and his re-assignment," he whispered to his friend. "Also, the prayers are more distracting than inspiring. I prefer the teamwork and sense of purpose that the ONB paramilitary training gives me."

"I see it in your eyes, your words. You love your new family."

During the late 1920s to the early 1930s, Venice became a case study in the promise of fascism. Strong national pride translated into massive recon-struction efforts, in which Marcello participated. He marched among the other Black Shirts in the rally on November 4, 1929, "Vittoria Veneto day," in the Giardinni Pubblici at the Colonna Rostrata that launched the Venice reconstruction efforts. Some of these efforts were showcases, such as expanding the large promenade along the Bay of San Marco, with Church of San Giorgio Maggiore across the waterfront (Riva degli Schiavoni) to the end of Via Garibaldi towards Sant'Elena. Marcello landed a job assisting with the renovation of Nicelli Airport, located on the Lido, the airport D'Annunzio and his squad flew missions out of during the war.

Each day as he came to study, Marcello passed the fresco by Mario Sironi depicting "Venice," "Italy," and "Study" in the Great Hall at the Venice University, Ca' Foscari. The fresco mirrors the fascist slogan, *Libro e moschetto, fascista perfetto*, or "Book and rifle, perfect fascist." The renovations to the entry included a fascist-oriented bas-relief heralding Venice as an epicenter of sea, art, and trade. Marcello marveled at these works of art.

Having completed his primary studies, Marcello worked on various projects around Venice that were part of the wave of infrastructure investments Mussolini had made to restore and rebuild Italy as a beacon of architecture and culture.

"Each brick, each pouring of concrete is an opportunity for me to give a piece of myself to Italy and to honor the memory and sacrifices of my parents. It does not matter what chore or effort the foreman assigns, I'll complete the task as if I own the road, the building, the wall."

Marcello studied while also practicing his acting. In 1933, Marcello attended acting master's class at Ca' Foscari and in 1935, he scored an uncredited extra part in the Guido Brignone film production about rebuilding a nation and a being proud fascist, *Passaporte Rosso.*

"They may not know my name now," he told his friends, "but they will. My heyday will come. I remain determined to be the next D'Annunzio."

For Marcello, the clouds of Sicily were far behind him. He soared high above Venice, like that Lanner falcon, his blue eyes glinting, all of Venice and Italy his prey, his playground. Marcello gave no indication anything could stand in his way. His virility and hope emanated like rays of sunshine, a veritable rapture, an undeniable presence capturing attention whenever he entered a room. Marcello's blue eyes sparkled beneath his wavy black hair with a piercing, vibrant intensity.

He enjoyed many lovers, but the lightning spark he felt when meeting another student, a dark-haired, spirited piano virtuoso studying at Foscari, captured Marcello's heart. The future held much promise indeed.

Areas of Italy

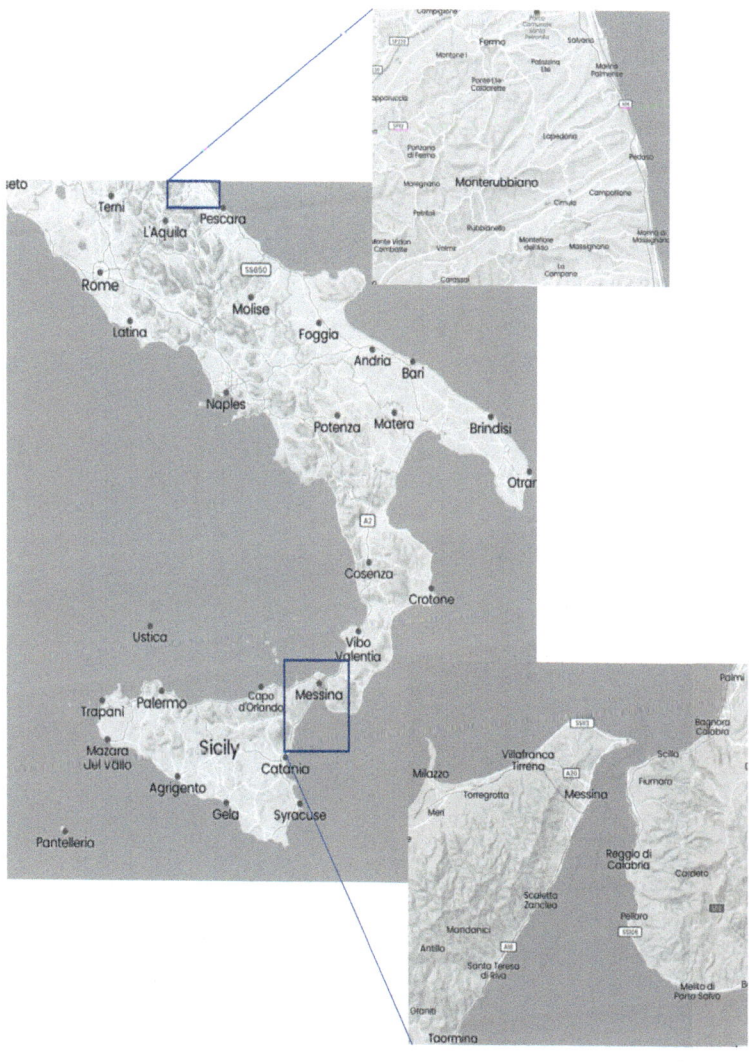

CHAPTER 2

Arrivederci, Italia e Maria-Luisa La Madre

*P*aolo di Vercellini worked hard, but while he did not have a formal education, he often demonstrated practical intelligence. He relied on the lessons learned on the farm as well as from his father. As all men of a certain age in Turin, he began military training, distinguishing himself for his verve and understanding of battle tactics. He lost no time moving up the ranks of the Piedmontese army, which led him to the inner circles of high society and exposed him to matters of finance.

In 1858, he earned the title "Marchese," granted by King Vittorio Emmanuel II in honor of his service. Marchese di Vercellini became the progenitor of a line of nobility within Turin high society that exercised influence and commanded respect throughout the late 1800s.

Given his lack of formal education, he determined that no other members of his family would face similar challenges or limitations on their future. He would therefore assure they were educated enough to expand on the wealth he amassed. Besides his emphasis on school and education, the Marchese was an avid patron of the arts, especially music. He often invited friends and consignment-composers, such as Paolo Giuseppe Ghebart and Giovanni Bolzoni, to the estate where attendees and performers alike socialized in the grand hall.

Marchese di Vercellini vacationed with his wife, Maria Fabioneta and family at their villa on the island of Stresa on Lake Maggiore. The parapet of the east tower offered sweeping views across the lake.

"I enjoy how this panorama captures the radiance of the sunset," she told him.

He nodded. "Yes, it's a view that affirms my love for God and for my Italy."

His financial dealings were as lucrative as his exploits on the battlefield were convincing. In addition to financial wealth, di Vercellini fathered five children in all, three sons and two daughters. As a family, they spent many months at Stresa.

The boys paddled about the lake, swimming or fishing, while the daughters went swimming or played their version of hide-and-seek with the other girl children of the servants and keepers who travelled with the Marchese and his family.

Maria sighed. "The sound of children playing mixes into the sound of the wind coming across the lake and mingles with the leaves during the change of seasons." Smiling, she turned to Paolo. "It brightens the sunshine glistening off the water."

Commander Giuseppe Garibaldi often visited with di Vercellini. Marchese di Vercellini held great respect for Garibaldi, which allowed them to maintain a long relationship that spanned the many incarnations of Garibaldi's life across multiple continents. They often engaged in lengthy, sometimes heated but always entertaining, exchanges about battle tactics, politics, the economy, government and Mazzini and the nationalist movement to unify Italy.

"I'm sure the neighbors across the water can hear your rough voices and excited intonations late at night," Maria said in a chiding tone, "as you share all those robust glasses of wine."

"All we do is interrupt the crickets or frogs that compete for attention."

One night, after the wine gave way to their new taste for the recent creation, Sambuca, Garibaldi hatched a plan. "Paolo, do you recall that young man and officer I brought with me a few times before, Federico Moresco?"

di Vercellini paused, reflected and nodded. "Yes, a handsome, polite young man. Seems to be intelligent, sharp and knows his place well."

Garibaldi smiled. "It's no secret I favor him and have been mentoring him." He paused before continuing, his words to be chosen with care. "Paolo, what do you think about introducing him to Barbara?"

Paolo pursed his lips, saying nothing.

"I'm sure many suitors must admire your eldest

unmarried daughter, Barbara Maria. Her long wavy black hair, fair complexion, high cheek bones and position in society make her one of the region's most desired debutantes."

"I required that Barbara received formal training in the arts and music," Paolo said. "I hired a private tutor to teach her sciences, literature and math." He paused to take another sip of wine. "You must also be aware that her intelligence as well as her beauty are intimidating. Most of the young men calling on my daughter lack the verve required to meet my standards."

He turned to Garibaldi, grinning. "But you know, Giuseppe, that is not one of your worst ideas."

The plan was hatched; Garibaldi conspired with di Vercellini to introduce Barbara Maria to Federico.

The courtship began with chaperoned walks around the gardens of the di Vercellini estate. Federico Moresco attended formal conversations with Barbara in their salon, under the watchful eye of her mother. The conversations were timely and political, sometimes about the flowers or the weather, but for the most part, testing each other's thoughts or philosophies on relationships and family. Garibaldi and di Vercellini noted the progress of the relationship with amusement.

"I am pleased with Moresco," Paolo whispered to Maria in private. "I hope he will be the next son-in-law."

Within ten months of meeting, Federico and Barbara were married.

* * *

In 1859, King Emanuel II appointed Count Camille de Cavour as Prime Minister and Garibaldi as Commander of the army to lead the Piedmont push against the Habsburg's and Austrian rule in the northern part of the peninsula along the foothills of the Alpine mountains. With the support of Napoleon as well as the French, Garibaldi and his troops were successful at liberating the Piedmont region.

After that victory, he set off for Sicily with 1,000 volunteers to recruit an army on Sicily and begin the unification of Italy from the south. He ferried his men from Genoa to Marsala to stage his invasion of the Kingdom of the Two Sicily's, ruled by a Spanish Bourbon and an ally to the Habsburg regime. He lost no time in gaining support from locals as he moved from Palermo across the island and onto the mainland, rapidly pressing toward Naples.

Meanwhile, the rest of the Piedmont army, including Moresco, pushed along the northern borders and to the south and east, attacking the Duke of Parma (a Habsburg) and the Duke of Tuscany (a Bourbon as well), closing the gap while accelerating towards Garibaldi, meeting up just north of Naples, at Teano.

Moresco's troop, led by King Emmanuel, were instrumental in the revolt against the forces defending the papal state in the Marche, Umbria and Abruzzo regions along the Adriatic to the east of Rome.

The year 1870 marked the completion of the risorgimento, the unification of Italy, to include Rome, while the Papal state of the Vatican remained independent. This also signaled the natural conclusion to Moresco's military career. His travels and battles had taken him from Turin, across the Italian peninsula, through the Marche region along the Adriatic and southwest toward Naples. He knew one day he would return to the le Marche. As he surveyed the verdant valleys, sweeping landscapes and majestic mountains, with the Adriatic-borne breeze, Federico felt a sense of destiny. Soon afterward, he prepared to settle in the region with his wife to start a family.

* * *

"Where are we going?" Barbara said to Federico as they oversaw the packing of their belongings. "What's it like there?"

"My estate is located near Monterubbiano, in the province of Fermo, south of Ancona and to the east of Monte Vettore and Monte Priora, in the foothills of the Sibillini Mountains. It is a small town, near the equally small seaside community blessed with pebbly alabaster shores of Pedaso on the Adriatic Sea."

"My father says they produce excellent wines there due to the hilly terrain and temperate climate."

"Yes, you'll see vineyards with Sangiovese and

Montepulciano grapes, along with chestnuts and truffles."

As they approached, Barbara gazed at the rich grasses covering the hills and plains. "See how it ripples in the wind, like waves!"

"Yes, it provides an abundance that supports goats, sheep and cattle, which in turn produce world-renowned cheeses. The mountains and forests are filled with wild game."

"So, I guess you and your guests will be hunting often," she said with a sigh.

An accomplished austringer, he admitted he planned to let his European Sparrowhawk prey on the local wildlife.

Federico Moresco and his family grew wealthy in their own right, producing highly sought-after leathers, selling their grapes to local vintners and producing a regional award-winning pecorino cheese. The di Vercellini blood lines, with familial support, secured favorable finances and mentoring to grow their estate and business. The number of employees expanded dramatically. Their success is a legacy; the town of Moresco lies just outside of Monterubbiano.

Moresco's youngest son, Giuseppe, named after his mentor, Garibaldi, was born in 1875. His father decided to raise him in the family business from an early age. He continued to build their empire and economic legacy of his father, leveraging his education from universities in Turin and Rome that the di Vercellini family ties still provided. He and his wife,

Augusta, struggled to raise healthy children, losing three in their infancy to sickle cell disease.

Then, in 1913, Guiseppe was called to the house from work. The doctor informed him Augusta had given birth to a daughter.

"Will she survive?" Giuseppe whispered, glancing at Augusta, who lay pale and still with her eyes closed.

"Yes, your wife will recover," said the doctor.

"No, I... I mean, my daughter." He moved closer to the bed, staring at the infant. "Will she... suffer the same fate as the others?"

"Time will tell," said the doctor with a sigh. Then he picked up his black bag and left.

Augusta's eyes fluttered open. "I want to name her Maria-Luisa, after my grandmother."

Giuseppe's balance gave way and he staggered to the side of the bed, kneeling beside his wife. He bowed his head, intending to pray, but no words came out. Tears streamed down his cheeks, until Augusta laid her hand across the back of his head. She left it there until his sobbing ceased.

After she turned two years old, Maria-Luisa Moresco occupied a bedroom on the second floor of the family estate, one that overlooked the olive grove to one side and the central courtyard on the adjacent side. Light filled her room every day while a sea-kissed breeze, carrying wafts of the country and the seashore together in a harmonious dance, swirled through her room. Her long dark hair, fiery eyes, smooth olive complexion and beguiling smile were striking. Maria-Luisa glowed with a beauty mirroring the countryside she was born into.

Her grandfather, the Marchese himself, doted on her, remarking how much she resembled her grand-mother, who had died several years prior.

"You do not hide the fact that she is your favorite grandchild," said Giuseppe to him one day.

The Marchese shrugged. "She must feel a special bond with me as well. We spend time together in the kitch—"

"Yes, I hear about it. Making spaghetti and mussels or roasting a hare to have with her mother's fried tagliatelle. Augusta told me she laughs and squirms hysterically when you tickle her."

The Marchese nodded, smiling at his son.

"Once, Augusta told me, when you were together, Maria-Luisa laughed so hard she felt like she almost peed."

"Well, maybe." He paused. "When I pick her up to swing her about in the fragrant air of the groves, she says it feels as if she could fly."

Around the time Maria-Luisa turned four years old, her grandfather became quite ill and was no longer able to come visit from Turin.

"Nonno will miss my next birthday!" she wailed as she threw books, cups and bowls against the walls, smashing them to the floor, stomping the bits into dust, as she screamed and thrashed about.

"She is so temperamental, often too moody," her

father muttered to her mother one evening after dinner as they retreated into the parlor.

"At least Maria-Luisa channels her emotions into vigorous playing of the piano," Augusta said, pointing to her daughter seated at the instrument across the room.

"Good thing we discovered her talent at a young age," he grunted. "Now friends or family often request to hear her play."

Her piano occupied one corner in the parlor, a grand room with two sets of thick-paned double doors that opened onto the courtyard with pots of rosemary, dwarf lemon trees and gardenia, as well as a large fireplace with a two-meter-wide stone hearth. Her lessons filled the courtyard and echoed throughout the estate, enthralling the housekeepers, the kitchen staff and her parents, no matter where they were.

"We should nurture Maria-Luisa's piano virtuosity," said Augusta in a firm tone.

"How?"

"By enrolling her in a program in Turin."

"Turin? Where will she live in that city?"

"With the di Vercellini family."

And thus, it was decided. A few years later Maria-Luisa travelled to Rome with other members of the di Vercellini clan. In 1923, at the age of 10, Maria-Luisa auditioned for Ottorino Respighi, a piano composition teacher at the Conservatorio di Musica Santa Cecilia in Rome. She studied with him for a year before she then trained with Alfredo Casella, who taught piano at the Accademia Nazionale di Musica Santa Cecilia in Rome.

"You have so much beauty in you," Casella told Maria-Luisa, "and you must learn to bring it out."

He was an influential activist in the Italian music industry, founded an association to promote modern Italian music, the "Corporation of the New Music," in 1923, with D'Annunzio and Gian Francesco Malipiero from Venice.

"I'll always remember the fresco behind the organ at Santa Cecilia," Maria-Luisa said to her friends later, "a depiction of three people standing around a tree with horses and soldiers flanking them."

"Sounds lovely."

"I imagine that Casella, D'Annunzio and Malipero could have been those three people, defending the tree of musical knowledge and progress from those trying to attack it."

* * *

Life in Italy changed for Maria-Luisa in January 1925, when Mussolini became dictator. He launched his campaign to suppress activities and organizations that he considered undermined the state. "Everything in the state, nothing outside the state, nothing against the state."

The Black Shirts were introduced, extended arm salutes plus their songs were everywhere, while Mussolini's incantations mimicked what he had earlier witnessed D'Annunzio achieve in Fiume and Rome.

In 1926, Maria-Luisa enrolled in the ONB as a "young Italian," the name given to the age group of girls that were to be taught about taking care of a home, knitting and cooking. The ONB did not support girls thinking of careers outside of raising a family. Maria-Luisa hated every minute of it.

"I dream of a life far away from the ONB, the isolation of Monterubbiano," she told her friends, sneering as she spit out her words. "I have no interest in growing grapes or tending sheep or producing leathers or cheese. My love… my passion… will always be music. Anything that interferes with that will receive my wrath."

The restrictions of the Fascist ONB infuriated her, overshadowing even her love for the countryside, or the thrill at watching her father practice falconry with his Sparrowhawk, or the joy she experienced riding her horse across the Fermo countryside.

"Professor Casella, I seem to be in oppressive situation. Can you give me any ideas or recommendations about how to escape?" Gasping, she clutched her hand to her chest.

"Let me use my connections," he said, holding his palm forward in an attempt to calm her, "to get you into the summer programs with Edwin Fischer, a German pianist and music teacher who runs the Music Institute for Foreigners in Potsdam, near Berlin, at the Marmorpalais."

Maria-Luisa nodded.

"Your tutelage under Fischer will expand your understanding as well as your appreciation for German composers and build within you a strong affinity for composers such as Schumann and Chopin."

"Oh, thank you so much!"

True to his word, he contacted Fischer to schedule her tryout.

"I can compliment your good posture, along with your strong fingering to the keys," Fischer told her after hearing her perform for the first time. "You possess an excellent understanding of the phrasing and dynamics of the pieces you played."

Maria-Luisa attended summer sessions with Fischer from 1928 until 1931, at which time Fischer stopped the summer sessions, instead forming his own chamber orchestra. Then Maria-Luisa received a referral with a recommendation to further her studies with Arnold Schoenberg and Friedrich Wuhrer in Vienna.

"How well her temperament and playing styles pair with those of Mozart, Schumann, Brahms...," said Schoenberg.

"And also Schubert and Chopin," said Wührer, nodding.

Her didactic, regimented playing became more nuanced and reflective as she became influenced by the Second Viennese School (*Zweite Wiener Schule*), including Schoenberg's and Wührer's teachings.

Relentless in his method, Wührer dug into Maria-Luisa, drilling her non-stop to develop perfection in her phrasing and expression.

"Beethoven is persuasive, furious, sorrowful, cheerful, painful, but never mumbles!" he shouted at her. "He is not boring, yet you bore me now!"

Maria-Luisa understood his message as a plea for accuracy and energy, a balance in expression and interpretation. These lessons were foundational to her maturation as a concert pianist.

As her repertoire and reputation grew, so did the opportunities to perform. Maria-Luisa appeared with the Berlin Philharmonic, conducted by the German composer and conductor, Wilhelm Furtwängler, receiving her first recording opportunity in 1931, to accompany a young American violinist, Yehudi Menuhin. Menuhin had made several recordings with different piano accompanists under the guidance of his mentor, the Romanian composer and violinist George Enescu.

They recorded Edward Elgar's *Violin Concerto in B minor* with Maria-Luisa as his accompanying pianist. Menuhin and Moresco paired up again in Paris in 1934 with an Austrian violinist, Fritz Kreisler, to record Paganini's *D major Concerto* and to work with Pablo Casals, a Spanish cellist who was also a conductor.

* * *

Maria-Luisa's success created mixed emotions. The opportunities and professional freedoms she enjoyed were in stark contrast to the emerging realities of 1930s life in Germany and Italy. Many of her childhood friends, including friends of her family, across Italy were ostracized or they suffered verbal and physical abuse as the political tides continued toward fascism amid Mussolini's efforts to align himself with Hitler.

The shift and societal pressure seemed to escalate every year since 1929 when Mussolini agreed in the Lateran Accords to make Roman Catholicism the official religion of Italy. Thus, his antisemitism became apparent. So much so, that Augusto Terati, the Fascist Party Secretary, resigned in 1930 because of the shift in policies toward more authoritarian, violent means.

By 1933, fascist momentum manifested itself in a spectacle as Blackshirts marched into the Piazza Venezia in Rome, along with a throng of young, old, students, mothers and children, all pressed toward the balcony that Mussolini spoke from. His newspaper, *Il Populo d'Italia*, described the scene as "an immense religious rite of faith." The ovations after the speech were so thunderous that he returned to the balcony, waving to the adoring crowd, three additional times.

The crowd's zeal reflected the coordinated efforts between the Fascist government and the Vatican. The influence on the Italian and Catholic way of life from communism, Protestants and the Jews concerned the Vatican. Starting in the mid-1920s, Tacchi Venturi, a Jesuit emissary of Pope Pius XI, initiated a conspiracy theory that the Jews, Masons and Protestants were a threat to Christianity and Italy. In 1928, Pope Pius XI made a speech forbidding Catholics from interfaith dialog. He also stopped the outreach to Italian Jews, as well as all conversion efforts.

The conspiracy theorists fanned the flames of discontent and mistrust by spreading additional rumors. One rumor implied the Jews were the reason for the Bolshevik revolution, creating a direct link between Jews and societal unrest.

The rumors had an effective impact on both public opinion and government policy. In March 1933, a high school in Turin, with a significant number of Jewish students, sought permission to allow the city's chief rabbi to offer religious education to these students. The Pope, through his emissary, Cardinal Pacelli, informed Mussolini that this should not be acceptable. Mussolini's government stepped in to revoke the Turin high school's authorization.

Social tensions in central Europe continued to escalate. Edith Stein was a German philosopher living in Munich, Jewish by birth, but converted to Christianity in 1923. Alarmed by the rising tension, she wrote a letter in 1934 to Pope Pius XI, begging for his public condemnation of the Nazi campaign against the Jews.

He ignored her letter. Rather, Pope Pius XI, concerned about the anti-Catholic actions of the Nazi movement, wanted Hitler's assurance that the persecution of Catholic priests would stop. He also sought to affirm Hitler's support, implied in a speech Hitler gave to German bishops, where he positioned the persecutions as a service to the Church, providing an answer to the "Jewish problem," aiding them in the Church's 1,500-year-old battle.

Not only were Pius' objectives not achieved, but Nazi persecution of German monks and nuns on charges of sexual perversion, including their abuse of children, accelerated. By 1936, the persecution of German clergy received wide-spread press coverage. The Nazis captured Edith Stein in a convent in the Netherlands in 1942. She died at Auschwitz.

In 1933, Schoenberg, a Jew forced to flee Germany, emigrated to the United States. Furtwängler, who stayed in Germany, became very controversial with an outspoken stance against Hitler's social policies. At the same time, he participated in events for the Nazi party while being part of the political propaganda.

Maria-Luisa remained in touch with Wührer but watched the antisemitism rhetoric coming from both Germany and Italy with grave concern. "I'm very worried for friends and family, especially in the Marche region with its large Jewish population," she told her friends. "Thousands of Jews have been told to emigrate, to leave Italy. I know several families both in the Fermo province and in Turin who chose to go to America. They refused to stay and face the increasingly difficult environment in Italy."

* * *

Today, the Jewish Heritage Route in Italy passes through twenty-five towns and cities in the region, including Monterubbiano.

However, one place seemed immune to the ongoing social changes and worsening, even chaotic, political environment – Venice. In 1930, Count Giuseppe Volpi di Misurata and Vittorio Cini, a wealthy industrialist, inaugurated the International Festival of Contemporary Classical Music as an extension of the Biennale Di Venezia celebration in Venice.

The energetic, vibrant Venetian life pulsed with color and rhythm. Tourists visited the beaches. Enthusiastic patrons attended annual music and film festivals. Football (soccer) tournaments and seasonal opera performances at Teatro Malibran continued without interruption. The city bustled with diners, students, politicians and actors, as well as the on-going construction of the Fascist-inspired rejuvenation.

* * *

In 1934, Maria-Luisa moved to Venice to pursue advanced master studies in composition and piano at Ca'Foscari. Shortly after arriving there, Maria-Luisa performed with orchestras both in Rome and Venice. While at Teatro Reale in Rome, she met Tullio Serafin, an Italian conductor who had been the Musical Director at La Scala Opera house in Milan. That year, Serafin was the artistic director of the Teatro Reale in Rome.

On weekends and after classes, Maria-Luisa and her girlfriends frequented many of the bars and clubs around Venice. One evening, in 1935, they attended a university-sponsored play loosely based on the movie, *Passaporte Rosso*.

"Oh, we can see that among all the performers, Marcello Carnabuci has captured your attention," one of her girlfriends said in a teasing tone.

Another one clutched her hand to her chest and took two whirling dance steps. "Something about the way he speaks mesmerizes me, his delivery hypnotizing."

They all laughed.

But Maria-Luisa could not deny that his passion and energy called to her in a way she never experienced before.

As Marcello came on stage that night, he noticed in the second or third row a ravishing, beautiful woman, her facial features somewhat illuminated by the stage lights, the shadows unable to mask the intensity of her gaze or the purposefulness presentness in her posture. He almost forgot his lines that evening.

After the performance, Marcello watched as Maria-Luisa congregated with her girlfriends on the steps of the theater. For a half-second, he detected his stomach in his throat and a nervousness not felt in a long time. He hesitated, blushing.

"You are good on stage, but you are not ready for life," Maria-Luisa said as she gave him a sly smile.

Maria-Luisa was quite a bit shorter than Marcello, a detail he could not discern from the muted stage lighting, but she seemed so much bigger now. Her opening invitation amplified his hesitation and awkwardness, which he struggled to conquer.

"Is it better to speak nonsense or to be purposeful, to know fully what you are about and what you want?" To underscore how irritated he was, his tone was sharp, yet also a bit lilting to express his hopefulness and intrigue.

"So, what do you want, since you seem so purposeful?" She spun on her heel to turn and face him as she and her girlfriends descended the stairs.

"You will all come to our after-show party. You, plus your friends." Marcello called after her, as he regained his composure and asserted himself.

"Given your obvious Sicilian roots," she said with a twinkle in her eyes, "I grant you pardon for your somewhat bold, aggressive style. So, yes, we will come to your party."

Almost without hesitation, Marcello and Maria-Luisa began a blazing hot, passionate affair. Marcello admired her beauty, especially her facial features, glossy black hair and piercing black eyes. Her exactness and unwavering discipline in music impressed him. Her capacity for love together with her passion, as expressed through her music as well as her kiss, seemed to have no bounds. He fell in love with this intense woman. She felt the same about him.

Maria-Luisa found Marcello to be a charming romantic, though perhaps also a bit too full of fantasy, also a bit too frivolous for her more German-oriented training. His poetic way of seeing things, his perception of beauty, his passionate, energetic being opened her heart, charging her with an electric sensation and boundless desire.

Marcello and his friends joined Maria-Luisa's troupe, dancing and dining at the hottest Venetian spots. Dance clubs or music performances were favorites.

In May 1935, Maria-Luisa received an invitation. "I've been asked to a performance in Vienna given by my prior teacher, Friedrich Wührer. He's performed with the Max Strub Trio."

"Who is that?" Marcello said as he twisted a strand of her hair around his finger.

"Max Strub is a German violinist of world renown, started his fame with Fischer's chamber orchestra before forming his own trio with Friedrich Wührer on the piano and Paul Grümmer on the cello."

Marcello and Maria-Luisa attended the performance. Afterward at the post-performance party, Wührer introduced Moresco, then aged twenty-two, to Strub, who was thirty-five.

Maria-Luisa, in one of the few times in her life where she found herself at a loss for words, hesitated, then said, "Your performance was very moving, very emotional. I could tell the music meant something to you."

Strub gave her a quick smile. "I am not accustomed to such boldness, nor being exposed for my vulnerability. However, I find your shyness… or perhaps even embarrassment, endearing."

Later, Wührer said to Strub, "I could not help but remark on the demeanor and instant rapport between you, truly remarkable."

"Yes, she is impressive in her own right," said Strub, "and I will endeavor to maintain a friendship there as I navigate these new waters."

A few years had passed since Strub's separation from his wife and his subsequent nervous breakdown. "She has a warmth, a genuineness" said Strub, "I find it comforting in some ephemeral, cathartic, perhaps even medicinal, manner."

Marcello and Maria-Luisa's passion for life, music and each other also extended to lengthy debates about fascism's impact on Italy.

"Your strong, pro-Fascist sentiments" she told him, "conflict with my concern about the impact of the changes in Italian politics on my long-time friends. I am distressed by the loss of liberties and diversification I believe in."

Their heated political exchanges took on new weight in 1936 when Mussolini, seeking to advance his political agenda and gain status with Germany, declared support for the Nationalist faction leader, General Francisco Franco, against the Spanish Republic in the Spanish Civil War. The Italian press reported on attacks on Spanish clergy, where hundreds were killed and churches were set ablaze. The press also inflamed Italian sympathies for the rebels fighting against the Spanish government when Russia flew in supplies to support the government.

The Italian Catholic Press urged Mussolini to send Italian troops to support the rebels. He listened, recruiting for the Corps of Volunteer Troops (*Corpo Truppe Volontarie*). The CTV was predominantly Voluntarii Littorio, volunteers inspired by the ONB. The ONB sponsored paramilitary training for years and graduates like Marcello were eager to use that training to perform their duty for their country.

Maria-Luisa told Marcello, "I do not consider your ONB training to be useful in your preparation as a soldier. Going to Spain to fight makes me nervous."

They went together to Nicelli Airport, the same airport D'Annunzio flew out of. Now Marcello, flushed with pride and enthusiasm, also departed from this infamous airport. She felt desperate to share a secret with Marcello. Despite many opportunities to do so on the way to the airport, even during the days leading up to his flight, she kept quiet instead, stewing in her anger and frustration, reluctant to face such deep fear and anxiety that overwhelmed her.

Marcello boarded his plane, waving and exuberant, smiling, his other arm around other volunteers he had befriended in the ONB. Maria-Luisa waved, unable to stop crying. In her letters to Wührer and Strub that February, she expressed her concerns and misgivings.

The victory in Malaga, their first offensive since landing in Spain, emboldened Marcello and the other Blackshirts of the CTV. Mussolini sent regular Italian army to augment their forces with orders to advance to their next objective, an offensive on Madrid. The Italian forces were a combination of Italian army and ONB paramilitary-trained volunteers. Some other volunteers joined them, tricked into coming to Spain, believing they were headed to Africa as movie extras.

The Italian troops assembling the morning of battle were in chaos, orders yelled over one another, soldiers scrambling to find their unit. Some volunteers, ones who had been duped about the nature of their service, realized the truth and ran away.

The Republic forces, with support from Russian

military and tanks, mobilized in the surrounding countryside in anticipation of the attack, as they expected a siege on Madrid. The unorganized, frenetic movement of the Italian troops raised an alarm with the Republic troops.

Just outside of the city limits of Madrid, the Italian fighting forces encountered the regular Army troops of the Spanish Republic at the Battle of Guadalajara, on the 8th of March 1937. As the Italians mobilized their march toward Guadalajara, the Republic troops launched a mortar barrage, while the tanks bombarded the approaching troops and roadway.

Marcello's unit was in disarray, bodies partially blocking the road ahead. The ones bleeding screamed, while the smoke and smell of burnt flesh overwhelmed Marcello's senses, already stunned by the thunderous explosions roiling the ground around them.

Bewildered and dazed, Marcello halted where he stood, unable to react to the high pitch scream of the incoming ordinance. The explosion knocked him off his feet, propelling him fifteen feet to the left. The shrapnel sheared off his right leg and arm.

Marcello did not return to Venice and Maria-Luisa.

Map of Venice

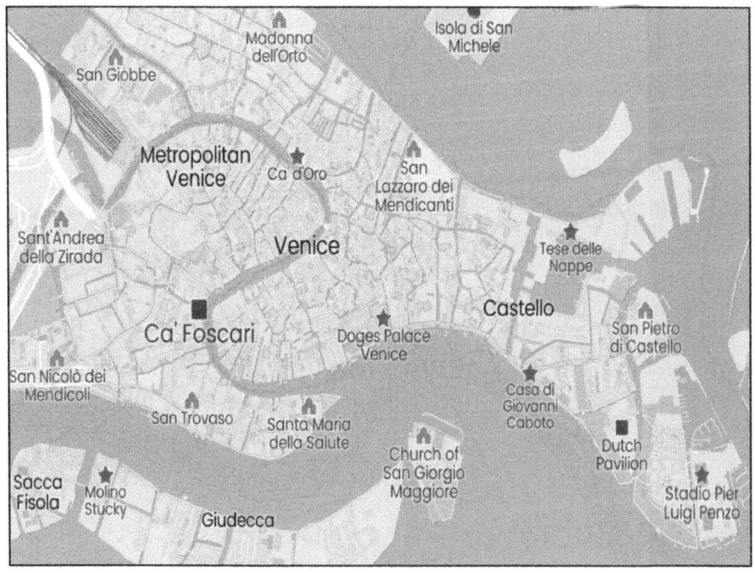

CHAPTER 3

Champagne e Guerra, Madre e Figlia

aria-Luisa had not told Marcello about the pregnancy. The news of his death brought back the pain of her grandfather. She let loose a long guttural scream, pounding her fists against the wall. She overturned furniture and screamed once more. As destructive as she felt in that moment, it only reflected a small fraction of the true rage and resentment boiling inside her.

Maria-Luisa maintained a small flat in Venice throughout the pregnancy, uncertain what to do next, only knowing her Catholic faith and the sanctity of becoming a mother. Relatives and friends back in Turin and Monterubbiano offered their assistance, but she did not want to give up on her piano or music career aspirations to settle into court life.

Max Strub came to visit Maria-Luisa often, in between performances with his newest trio, including pianist Elly Ney and the cellist Ludwig Hoelscher. His preparation of a Brahms' violin concerto for his soloist debut with the Berlin Philharmonic kept him practicing, even during visits.

"I treasure Max's presence, given his experience of three children from his first marriage," she told herself. "He also keeps the dream of music alive in my heart."

In the weeks leading up to the delivery, Maria-Luisa put the finishing touches on the changes to her apartment. A crib gifted from her aunt in Turin proved too large for her nursery. She sold it to a shop around the corner on Calle de Corli, then purchased a smaller, less ornate one. Rattles and toys lay in baskets nearby, some from family and others from friends. A mosquito net that Max hung from the ceiling created a lace tent around the crib. Soft cotton washcloths and diapers were piled in another basket next to the crib.

Augusta, Maria-Luisa's mother, arrived in Venice during the late fall of 1937. She entered the apartment with caution, surveying the rooms, in silence observing the creases in the curtains, the organization of the kitchen, the air and light and space for the child. Her eyes scanned the walls, the floors, at last settling on her daughter for the first time since Maria-Luisa had left for Venice.

Polite letters along with occasional calls had helped to maintain awareness. Augusta chafed at the obstinance of Maria-Luisa regarding her music. Her insistence on a woman having her own career incensed Augusta. Who did she think she was, after all?

She disgraced the court life and tradition of raising children in the Italian way. The Filangieri followed this tradition for centuries. As did the de Vercellini family. Did she not know how precious this moment is, how wonderful this opportunity, plus how much pain she and Giuseppe endured through the miscarriages before being blessed with Maria-Luisa? Now, Maria-Luisa proposed to raise this child in this hovel, the stench of the canals barely tolerable, the heavily filtered light unable to discern time of day. Not a tree or songbird in sight. Perhaps she would change Maria-Luisa's mind.

Without her mother saying a word, Maria-Luisa discerned what Augusta thought. Maria-Luisa whirled around and stepped back from the entry where Augusta stood for mere precious seconds. In frosty silence she communicated her sentiments back to Augusta, with only a look, in a way that polite words over the telephone or in letters could never convey.

Mid-morning a few weeks later, Maria-Luisa's water broke while she stood in the kitchen making an espresso. Her mother dashed to the kitchen, called for the ambulance and assisted Maria-Luisa to a chair. The ambulance arrived within a few minutes, yet the contractions were still several minutes apart. They raced to Giovanni e Paolo Hospital, where Maria-Luisa was rushed to a delivery room, her mother close behind.

The uncomplicated delivery finished within the

hour. Chiara Barbara Maria Francesca Augusta Fabioneta Moresco was born on November 11, 1937.

After cleaning and wrapping Chiara in a swaddling, the nurse handed the child to her mother. Propped up on the bed, exhausted from the swift ordeal, Maria-Luisa received Chiara with tremendous trepidation. She shifted her arms and shaking hands under the bundled child, attempting to understand this new reality as much as she struggled to hold Chiara. She fumbled to open her gown to allow Chiara to take a nipple in her mouth. When Chiara clamped down on her breast, she gasped, dropping the baby into her lap, spraying milk across her face. They both cried in that moment.

Maria-Luisa believed that in life, like in music, patience is needed to differentiate between a moment that has emphasis or persuasion and a moment that has significance or determination. The birth of Chiara was one of these moments when Mara-Luisa needed to pause, to reflect about whether being a mother would determine and define her, or if it would be a moment of emphasis.

And here, mere seconds into her life, she dropped her daughter. A defining moment indeed, thought Maria-Luisa.

No amount of discussion with Max had prepared Maria-Luisa for the reality of Chiara's first month.

"Each diaper change feels as if it happened mere minutes since the prior one," she whined. "I get no interlude, no break, an unrelenting assault on my senses."

She winced with the discomfort of her sore breasts. Chiara cried, likely from colic, at all hours of the day. Maria-Luisa felt the exhaustion in her shoulders as she tried to hold Chiara. She felt it in her back when she tried to change Chiara. She felt it in her temperament as she recoiled from the putrid stench that unpinning the diaper produced. The occasional gurgle or gleeful babble provided inadequate recompense for the toll exacted.

"We both sleep a bit better when I drink a glass of wine or two."

Too many glasses of wine, however, brought up memories of Marcello and his insistence to join the fight. His stubbornness. Her resentment at his abandoning her to do all this alone now. Her fears that having a child would sink her profession. Her rage at his selfishness. At her feelings of inadequacy.

She slammed the doors of the apartment as she moved about, the third glass of wine in one hand as she picked up items for the laundry, put away baby things, looked in the mirror to fix her hair or put on lipstick, as if expecting a different life to knock on the door and invite her to go there instead.

Mother and daughter often passed out on the couch, both physically and emotionally exhausted, lulled by the effects of wine.

The crying and babbles soon became a high-pitched screech and torrents of tears as Chiara strove to communicate with her mother. Maria-Luisa, however, sank into shorter temper, her nerves frayed by the continuous attention and care Chiara seemed to need. Chiara often pushed away or flailed her arms in disapproval at mashed vegetables or oatmeal.

When this happened, Maria-Luisa grabbed Chiara's wrists with a red face and boiling blood, holding her still, pushing her face close to Chiara's. Inches away, Maria-Luisa let loose with all the air in her lungs with force and intent.

This child will not get the better of me. I will not allow it.

Chiara's displeasure for mashed beets or peas or potatoes turned to fear and terror at the looming reddened face and bulging eyes that now towered over her. The bowl's contents on the floor, both mother and daughter cried in those moments, moments that collected like so many movements in an orchestral score.

Max continued his visits to Venice to see Maria-Luisa during the spring of 1938. He also arranged for a studio piano to be moved into the apartment for Maria-Luisa. Playing eased her tensions and she no longer depended on a glass of wine to soothe her nerves. She found purpose in each keystroke, each an expression of language, emotion and vitality she so sorely missed.

Despite their continued frustration with Maria-Luisa's firm resolve to stay in Venice, Augusta insisted that she and Giuseppe help their daughter with rent plus other expenses. With Chiara now crawling about the apartment, Maria-Luisa grew tired of having to maintain constant vigilance in order to stop Chiara from putting things in her mouth or choking.

Augusta advocated for Maria-Luisa to hire a nursemaid to watch over Chiara and help raise her. Maria-Luisa interviewed dozens of candidates before finding a German woman with musical training and excellent references, besides the additional bonus of having parents who were teachers themselves.

With the nanny hired, Maria-Luisa devoted even more time and attention to renewing her relationship with music and with Max, allowing her to re-engage with the Venetian musical society she so desperately missed.

Chiara seemed to intuit when her mother left her for too long and figured out how to get her back. She now understood the silent language her mother used, the different facial expressions and what they meant. Despite Maria-Luisa's reprimands or corporal discipline, Chiara developed a defiant resiliency, no longer flinching when Maria-Luisa grabbed her wrist, seldom crying if her mother used physical force.

Chiara liked to hear her mother play the piano. When Maria-Luisa went away with Max, the nanny allowed Chiara to sit on the bench and play with the keys of the piano. Chiara liked imitating her mother, perhaps looking for a bond with her as well.

Maria-Luisa, however, did not respond to her daughter's interest in the piano. "Encourage her interest," she told the nanny, "but proper training will begin only if Chiara continues to show aptitude at the age of four, the age when I committed myself to music. That litmus test will apply to my daughter as well."

In the spring of 1938, Maria-Luisa travelled with Max to Germany for his tour, providing her opportunity to discuss music with him, in addition to members of his trio, especially Elly Ney. The nanny cared for Chiara almost fulltime at this point. Max's presence entailed escorting Maria-Luisa to another party, or back to Berlin or to Weimar, Germany. His presence meant more time Maria-Luisa would be away from Chiara.

"I am excited to bring you to Weimar. My earlier life created such fond memories of Weimar, a storied, almost magical place in my heart. The community and society fostered an environment I want to share with you."

"After a few weeks with you, Max, the magic of Weimar has mesmerized me," she told him. "I've felt more at home with this society that cherished Strauss, Chopin, Mozart and Brahms the same way I do."

"Yes, it's difficult, if not impossible, to ignore the musical affinity and culture-driven magnetism of the region."

In the late spring of 1938, Maria-Luisa returned to Venice to retrieve Chiara and the nanny. They boarded the Venice train at Stazione di Venezia Santa Lucia rail station, leaving behind what little furniture she owned. Travelling with an infant necessitated at least one stop and overnight on the eighteen-hour journey.

Maria-Luisa gazed out the window of the train when it pulled away from Venice. The Alps loomed in the distance as they approached the mountain pass to leave Italy and cross the border of Slovenia and Austria.

"The trip already seems so long, so stifling," she said, her fingers tapping on the armrest in time with the clacking of the coach wheels on the rails.

The trio made their first stop at the point of transfer between the Italian rail and the German rail lines, in Villach, Austria. They arrived a few days after the Anschluss (the annexation of Austria by Germany) in 1938, streamers plus debris of the parade and celebration of the annexation still piled on the street, the notes of the German marching bands still ringing in the drunken heads of revelers.

As Maria-Luisa, Chiara and the nanny made their way from the Villach rail station to their hotel, they passed several German Color Guard troops posing for pictures with local Austrian women. Maria-Luisa tried to ignore world politics, in particular sentiments about the Germans.

"I understand why these historically German-speaking peoples retain their not-so-distant memories of greatness as part of the Prussian empire," she murmured to the nanny. "Still, I feel a bit of unease creeping into my heart, remembering the changes brought about by Mussolini's rise to power in Italy. I wonder how much adjustment Hitler will bring."

The time allotted for Chiara's rest, along with the break from arduous travel, ended a few days later. They boarded their next train in Villach, transferring once at the Salzburg station Schwarzach-St. Veit Bahnhof toward Munich before completing their journey and arriving in Weimar late in the evening.

* * *

Just to the south and west of Leipzig, Germany, the River Ilm meanders down first from the mountains, then through the valley. Its babbling waters, sensuous and intimate, varies in cadence as it wends its way, slow in places, rapid in others. The river visits each hill, caresses each pasture, interlaces with the arteries in the heart of Weimar.

Nature's grandeur is reflected in the deeds of those living there. Weimar claimed to be home for many famous artists, including the poet, Johann Goethe and the playwright, Friedrich Schiller. Weimar is where Johann Sebastian Bach performed as the court organist and concertmaster, composing some of his most famous choral preludes and cantatas. Richard Strauss and Franz Liszt also lived there, composing with their emotions and passions.

Forward-thinking architectural minds came to Weimar's Bauhaus school, inspired by residents Walter Gropius and Ludwig Mies van der Rohe.

Weimar is a city where nature and art fuse together as one, dancing along cobbled streets, whispering through ancient trees and storied alleys, breathing orchestral movements that play along to the rhythm of the Ilm's ribboned stanzas and where intellectuals absorb the energy born within the shadow of death.

The profound nobility of the Thuringian estates, its palaces with tall stone towers and gabled roofs, gilded halls lit by crystal chandeliers, fine silks mirroring the lush gardens, embodied the magical ambiance of the Ilm and Weimar. These estates of the wealthy and influential became the backdrop for the courtship between Max Strub and Maria-Luisa Moresco during 1937 and 1938.

Her daughter, Chiara, charmed everyone with radiant blue eyes against a frame of raven black hair. Chiara's *kindermädchen* watched over her, freeing Maria-Luisa to once again dream of living her life in music as well as society. From time to time, during the parties at the various schloss of the Weimar region, Maria-Luisa played a duet with Max's trio partner, pianist Elly Ney.

Ney was a celebrity in her own right, known by the title of "Professor" as honorarium bestowed by Adolf Hitler in 1937 to commemorate her birthday.

In the summer of 1938, Chamberlain Erich von Conta extended invitations to Schloss Kromsdorf for the "Swedish Festival," a celebration including music, hunting, eating and dancing, both in the palace and in their lavish gardens. Guests entered the estate through large, wrought iron gates anchored into thick stone walls. Parallel rows of enormous trees bordered the drive up to the schloss on either side, their overhead canopy framing the passage below.

As guests emerged from the shade, the palace shone bright in the late afternoon sun, reflecting off the white stucco in a dazzling, almost blinding manner. Several attendants manned the entrance at the white domed tower, parking arriving vehicles. Hand-carved stone frescos depicting animals in the hunt and the family crest surrounded over-sized, thick wooden doors. The heavy metal latch clanked as the lever was pressed. The door swung open with silent ease as guests entered the reception hall.

Large hand-hewn wood beams, shadowed recesses and vaulted corners decorated the reception hall's high cathedral ceiling. Crystal chandeliers descended from the dark to cast their light onto the red and gold baroque upholstered chaises and armchairs below. The ball-and-claw curved feet and ornate carved backs were austere enough to be elegant but not overstated. The polished granite floor, inlaid in a diagonal pattern, reflected ample light to give the room a warm glow. The walnut wainscot framed the hunt-and-garden-inspired silk tapestry on the walls. Their golds, hunter greens and deep reds allowed the silver and white accents to shimmer like ripples in a current.

Schloss Kromsdorf offered the Thuringian equivalent of a warm, comforting hug.

* * *

Maria-Luisa and Max accepted their flutes of champagne from the polished silver tray presented upon their entrance and were caught in the persistent current of arriving guests. They flowed towards the ballroom where the quartet the Chamberlain had engaged already played.

The grand ballroom's large open space, along with its tray ceiling painted with murals and clouds, exploded with colors of lapis blues and soft yellows, silver and white, bringing the sky and hope into the festive room. Maria-Luisa and Max stifled gasps as their eyes swept the room.

Flags, ribbons and fresh flowers burst from vases set on marble pillars. Guests formed eddies in the corners and around the floral displays, collecting among friends and acquaintances as the current carried them into and around the ballroom.

The two sets of French doors were cast wide open onto the garden beyond. The spring air rushed in as excited as the capriccio played by the quartet. Strub caught sight of Furtwängler across the room and headed off to talk with him. Maria-Luisa rushed to greet Wührer and Kreisler. Chiara went for a walk in the garden with her nanny.

The garden path began at the French doors, a stone trail leading to a tall ornate fountain with tessellating flower beds to either side. The garden's vibrancy mirrored the colors and energy of the ballroom, matching the hues and replacing the dynamics of the orchestra with the crescendo of petals waving in time with the breeze. Despite this grandeur, Chiara's kindermädchen preferred the more intimate, integrated garden at Weimar Schloss Belvedere.

"I enjoy Belvadere's garden with its wide paths, tall arbors and the boxwood rows that frame all those wonderful herbs," she said to the other nannies walking with their charges. "That garden invites me to sit, to take it all in, all those lovely stone statues surrounding that magnificent central fountain!" she gushed. "Last week was a nightmare with horrible weather during the party. We were forced to take shelter in the orangery. Since this little beast really liked the intense citrus scent and luscious greenery, she quieted right down," she continued, "which, as you all can attest, whatever can soothe these spoiled monsters becomes an instant favorite for me!"

While the nanny strolled about the garden with Chiara, Strub and Furtwängler meandered into Kromsdorf's hunting room where attendants served schnapps and beer. The massive room held many stuffed and preserved examples of hunts at Kromsdorf, as well as in the Alps, Russia and Africa. Tales about the lion skin on the floor or the full-size preserved Bengal tiger were mythological in proportion and boasting. The guests pooled in the vicinity of the tufted leather couches on either side of the open stone hearth, its small fire crackling, more for hypnosis than for warmth on that spring day.

Several top lieutenants and a few generals of the Third Reich were present, including Hermann Göring, dressed in military gray, metals attached to his chest, shoes polished to a mirror perfection. He leaned against the wall, staring down into the fire, a drink in his other hand, the flickering flames distorting his square jaw and deep-set eyes into a fearsome vision of intensity.

As Strub and Furtwängler entered, Göring, seeming to feel the internal flame of several schnapps, gesticulated mid-diatribe on his vision for what being a Nazi meant, about the inherent German lust for danger and adventure and his own specific passion for shooting, whether as an ace in World War I flying fighter aircraft or hunting wild game.

"I have a most urgent desire for an interesting hunt this afternoon," he said to the nonchalant Chamberlain, who surveyed the room as if to plan his escape. "I have, however, an expectation of disappointment, given the poor comparison of the woodland around Schloss Kromsdorf to my own hunting preserve at Schorfheide, even to the nature of the hall itself in comparison to Schloss Burgk an der Saale. Last week's hunt included one of my hunting partners, Lutz Heck."

"Ah, yes," said the Chamberlain with a slight nod, "the zoologist."

"Can you be honest," Göring said, "and tell me

that the hunting hall at Schloss Burgk an der Saale boasts a prodigious display of testosterone? I swear by the Führer himself, one could hardly imagine so drastic a difference from your hall and woods here from what is atop a hill only a few miles away."

His tone turned to taunting. "Do not mistake my admiration for Burgk an der Saale for any disrespect to your fine home here, Chamberlain, but you just have to admire those twin turret towers framing the south wall, how it overlooks the forest and lake with that damn bridge."

He paused to gaze at the ceiling, as if conjuring an image. "It is a downright castle with a moat. It makes me feel alive with the vitality, the verve of knights and queens, where the walls jut up out of rock as if they were a natural extension, part of the very rock they stand upon."

The Chamberlain hesitated as he took a deep breath to consider this debate with such a dangerous guest. "Yes, you are right," he said. "It is an impressive estate. I have forever admired its timber frame with its stucco exterior rising high above the surrounding countryside, exerting its dominance, both visually and emotionally. Yet while the stone walls and bridges are imposing, I have always been drawn to the craftmanship of the stone floors and carved arches inside, almost poetic how the cool grey slate stone floor in the entrance hall unfurled into the distance, flowing into rooms beyond through archways on both sides, as the Ilm cascades throughout our Weimar valley."

As he watched Göring relax a bit, the Chamberlain continued. "The domed ceiling of the entry, plastered and painted white, emblazoned with rococo-inspired gold leaf details, tracing from the corners to the center mural painted inside an ovel bas relief... it is all truly breathtaking. It is as close to divine inspiration as design and architecture can get."

Göring's eyes scoured the room the moment the Chamberlain started speaking, then feigned a modicum of interest once the Chamberlain shifted his analysis into the poetic realm versus expounding on the purely masculine theme he was focused on.

"Well said, Chamberlain," Göring shouted.

The Chamberlain clenched his jaw, assuming a neutral expression. When Göring ignored him, he studied the towering Siberian grizzly, erect with huge paws raised, regaining its ferocity. Antlers and horns surrounded the room. Mounted over the expansive hearth, its head turned toward the center, a red fox watched over the hall, its nervous glass eyes tracking those who smoked their cigars, drank their beers, schnapps, and in season, *gluwein*, as they retold stories of war and conquest.

"Regardless, you should be proud of your hall here as well," said Göring, looking to shift the conversation to something less interpretive.

When Göring noticed Strub and Furtwängler, he motioned for them to join him by the fire. Shaking their hands, he thanked them for their service to the arts and the purity of Ayrian ideals in the arts. "Most particularly your classic, true-to-origin interpretation of German music," he bellowed, then waved the back of his hand sideways to dismiss Strub, who edged away in silence.

Göring then turned his attention to Furtwängler. "I want to discuss with you upcoming events, especially the rallies that you will be responsible for composing and conducting."

Maria-Luisa flowed with the current of the afternoon's energy to the gallery. She observed a small group standing by one framed canvas displayed there, Simon Vouet's Allegory of Prudence. Maria-Luisa gazed at the painting of the woman with her mirror, the depictions of vices around her.

"I do not understand the allegory," said a rather tall, older woman whom Maria-Luisa recognized from previous parties. "Really, I think the painting is just not appealing to today's aesthetics and concerns."

"Oh Ella," said another, slightly younger and more fashionably dressed woman whom Maria-Luisa did not recall seeing before. "Do you not think judgment follows actions, regardless of past, present, or future? Are we not all subject to the judgment of time? Is this woman looking at her reflection seeing her past or is she trying to see her future? Has she been prudent, or is her prudence the moderation of the vices? Use your imagination!"

"Always with the attitude, Ida," snorted Ella, "but look here, the artist has listed vanity, greed, materialism, power and corruption. These are vicissitudes afflicting higher classes, wealth and power, the political and the industrial. What does the factory worker know of power or corruption, other than what he sees in others? These vices may be much more prevalent to a monarchy, which were also more pervasive in Vouet's era."

Maria-Luisa listened with interest. "Maybe," she said as she leaned her head toward them, "Vouet wants the viewer to look in the mirror, like the woman in repose glancing at her mirror, to see our 'true nature' as being something both beautiful as well as tempted, or even manipulated."

Ida and Ella nodded, contemplating Maria-Luisa's comment.

The Chamberlain's wife said, "We do not always make the right decisions, even if we believe we are acting with care and awareness, whether these vices or others. This is why I love this piece so much. It sparks a debate!"

Maria-Luisa found the conversation disquieting. Staring in the mirror, she thought, I have deceived myself about Max and Chiara. I have not been 'aware' or acting with purpose. I have ignored the rocky, turbulent rapids of my relationships with Max and Chiara.

She sighed as she studied the painting. The woman gazing into the mirror appeared graceful and peaceful. A blissfulness that she did not seem to have, not since Chiara. "I damn the day I met Marcello, he with his uncompromised life and me saddled with the responsibility he left behind!" Maria-Luisa wondered if she now pursued some desired but imagined and near impossible-to-achieve life.

Her face darkened with a shadow of depression and disillusion. "Who do I see in the mirror? A concertmaster pianist, or a mother?"

Max came alongside Maria-Luisa and slipped his arm around her waist. Her dark eyes locked his with a sense of hope accompanied by a sense of loss.

In the distance, the quartet began a Mozart waltz. They strolled back, through the hall. The music grew as they neared. Tuxedos and gowns swirled, while heads bobbed to mimic the composed lilt. The diffused orange-purple glow of sunset crashed through the windows and doors facing the garden. The now chilling twilight breeze tempered to perfection the massed body heat in the ballroom. The iced champagne and rosy cheeks of the many guests at Schloss Kromsdorf that summer day in 1938 set the standard for the Weimar party season ahead.

The dazzling party scene played out time and again as the elite moved up and down stream, following the Ilm in and around Weimar from Tiefurt to Burgk to Ettersburg to Belvedere and back again. The Ney trio played at a few of the parties that summer, with Maria-Luisa joining Ney as an accompanying pianist.

At times, when certain moments triggered memories of time spent in Weimar with his first family, Max turned melancholy, then nostalgic. They had spent summers in Weimar, visiting the family of Max's Jewish ex-wife, Hilde Neuffer, who had grown up in Weimar with her father, an actor and her mother, a writer. Max and Hilde had two children before their divorce in 1932; their daughter, Elgin, became a writer and later married John Ronayne, the concertmaster of the Bavarian Radio Symphony Orchestra. Their son, Harald, who showed signs of prodigy at age fifteen in 1938 as a cellist, joined the Arriaga Quartet, among other successes in his life.

While talking with Furtwängler that summer, Max reflected on the irony of being in Weimar again, with a new family, walking in the steps of his first family. "Wilhelm, I am struggling, I know Maria-Luisa and Chiara are unique to themselves, but I really just wanted to regain that peaceful existence I knew prior to the divorce and breakdown. I think I may have gone into this with some expectation they would be who I needed them to be."

Wilhelm pondered this for a moment, before countering, "I don't know, Max, maybe you should not be so hard on yourself. Of course, some part of you needed to escape the difficult acknowledgment of failure of that first marriage... sure, being with a younger woman is certain to give you a jolt of vitality. What is wrong with that? You deserve it." He clasped his friend's shoulder.

"I don't know, Wilhelm, I think I have been dreaming, these summer starlit nights and exuberance... yes, I feel young again but Maria-Luisa is not who I thought she would be."

"You make me laugh!" Wilhelm chuckled. "Of course, she appealed to your paternalism. She gave you something to fix, or focus on, rather than yourself. Therefore, you found tangible value through your caring and support."

Wilhelm paused a moment to stop laughing, but when he sobered up, he said, "Nothing here is a mystery... it is a tale as old as time itself. From what you have told me, in your very first meeting, before the other one died, you knew and understood her desire for music and were all too eager to help. Why do you feel guilt or remorse now, after you've realized your financial support would not help only Maria-Luisa? It would mostly be to validate yourself, Max, right?"

Wilhelm paused to gauge his friend's reaction. Shrugging, Max looked away, buried in his thoughts, as if searching for some answer that lay just beyond his grasp.

That June in a quiet ceremony, Max and Maria-Luisa married, surrounded by their friends and musical family.

"I prize the stability, the completeness the marriage gives to Chiara," Maria-Luisa admitted to one of her friends, "as well as the financial security and potential for exploring my professional ambitions."

Max saw the benefits of emotional support, comfort and companionship in an increasingly uncertain time. In that moment, at the end of the summer of 1938, Max could not appreciate how vast their respective faculties for love were, nor how intense their desire for love. Neither could he sense they were searching for different things. Maria-Luisa wanted to resume a path that had been diverted, so she shifted her attention and faculty for love to music and performing again. Max could not know what intense rejection and abandonment, directly and indirectly, he would feel.

"My fantasy is shattered for what I wanted her to be for me," he told Wilhelm.

As with the waning summer light that fall, the party ended and the rules changed.

The increasing amount of social and political conflict that summer cast a cloud over the party scene. The recent Mussolini publication of the Manifesto of Racial Scientists either appalled or amused guests in equal measure at the August soiree at the Tiefurt Mansion. The "scientific report" received significant press coverage in Italy. As published in La Civilita

Cattolica, Italians were identified as members of the Aryan race, with the specific denouncement of Jews not being Italian. The German people, especially the Third Reich members, did not consider Italians to be Aryan, no matter what Mussolini published.

The additional comments from Tacchi Venturi also received press coverage. He remained vocal about the need for restrictions to protect Christian society "from the noxious influence" of the Jews. The German press supported this stance, but many found Mussolini's actions to be ridiculous, a step too far. Everyone saw it as an obvious stretch of the imagination only to justify the alliance and allegiance to Hitler.

Some members of the Catholic Church also found the report disturbing, including Bishop Cazzani, because they saw Nazi-oriented racism as unjustified, even exaggerated. Such racism, their logic concluded, unjustly included Catholics, whereas Italians and Christian peoples were seeking to limit the "actions and influence" of Jews in order to minimize their influence on education or customs of Christians.

"I find neither stance acceptable,"Max said to Maria-Luisa in private. "We have both enjoyed long relations and deep friendships with many Jews."

"But we must also consider survival, especially for Chiara's sake," she said, shaking her head.

The cloak of secrecy and repression fomented an

undercurrent of fear, avoided at the galas, where the season's flow of champagne imitated the persistent current of the Ilm.

The Ettersburg Castle stuck an imposing, yet appropriate, backdrop for the final, end-of-season party. Its tall church steeple punctured the tree line, making it visible for miles. The main building stood to one side of the massive cobblestone paved quadrangle. This building offered the ballroom and main focal points for their entertainment. Ettersburg had evolved over time and now reflected a palace-within-a-palace construct. An existence within an appearance, not unlike Europe itself and the war-like atmosphere that was brewing.

Max and Maria-Luisa drove their Benz 770 along the drive toward the entrance, where attendants waited to park cars along the central courtyard. Halfway in, Göring sped past them in his Benz 540 Roadster, kicking up a cloud of dust and gravel.

"Let's promise each other to avoid him this time," Max said.

Maria-Luisa nodded.

When they arrived, Furtwängler greeted them, all but dancing with delight to show off his new powder blue Peugeot 402 Darl'mat Roadster. "I've been waiting all summer to get this car!"

"Well. the excitement on your face speaks testimony to your sense of triumph," Maria-Luisa said. "We give you our hearty congratulations."

Chiara seemed taken with the shiny new roadster. When her mother bent forward to admire the elegant interior, Chiara wriggled as she tried to peer at herself in the side mirror.

Furtwängler's giddy mood that afternoon dispelled the tensions caused by the recent German invasion and occupation of the German-speaking region of Czechoslovakia, named Sudetenland, along with the mobilization of French troops in response.

As Chiara's one-year birthday approached, Maria-Luisa and Max made preparations for her party. They invited guests to their home in Stuttgart.

On November 9th, however, their plans changed.

A Jewish teenager from Poland had killed a German diplomat in France on November 7th. By November 9th, a fervor escalated, stoked by pro-Nazi propaganda as well as inciteful rhetoric by politicians and news agencies in Germany. Riots erupted across Germany and Austria, dubbed *Kristallnacht*, or "night of broken glass." Synagogues were burned, Jewish stores were smashed and looted, hundreds of Jews were killed across Germany and Austria, while thousands more were rounded up and sent to concentration camps. Many more fled.

Instead of celebrating Chiara's first birthday, the family sequestered themselves in fearful anxiety. Max and the nanny joined Chiara and her mother for a more subdued, quiet, private moment. There were some balloons and a cake.

Chiara felt the attention on her in that moment. Giggling with excitement, she waved her hands above her head, knocking her spoon and milk over onto the floor. Max laughed.

When Maria-Luisa spoke her silent words, Chiara's exhilaration slipped away.

And in that moment, Maria-Luisa cast Chiara and all her youthful adventures alongside the crescendo of the swelling, supportive relationship that she had found with Max and the allegro tempo of high society life with all the praise and notoriety that it brought Maria-Luisa as a musician. Chiara instantly became a moment of secondary emphasis, if Maria-Luisa felt generous. A new determination welled inside her to build a different life for herself. The relationship with Max gave her the opportunity to establish that life. This awareness defined the beginning of the cadence and dissonance between Chiara and her mother.

Throughout 1939 and into 1943, Max toured, performing with the Elly Trio. From time to time, Maria-Luisa substituted for Ney or played along with Ney when they needed two pianos. Max earned the coveted role of Concertmaster of the Berlin Philharmonic and in 1942 performed Beethoven's Ninth Symphony, with Furtwängler conducting. The performance received accolades, setting in motion a decision to include Strub on the Gottbegnadeten list (also known as the "Führerliste") as one of the most important violinists in the Third Reich. This designation saved him from military service and gave him and his family freedom without question to travel across Germany to perform.

In October 1940, Maria-Luisa's father died in his sleep at the estate in Monterubbiano. Many changes had influenced the nature and spirit of the people in town since Maria-Luisa last lived there. Giuseppe shared his sadness over these changes when they talked. Frequent conversations helped them maintain a close relationship since she left for Venice several years ago. His health deteriorated over the years, but Maria-Luisa had planned to bring Chiara to see her grandfather in a few more months for her birthday. Now, the French and German troops were already engaged in combat. Travel to Italy became unsafe under any circumstance.

"I cannot accept his death as anything more than some surreal nightmare," she wailed, gushing tears. "I felt the same sense of loss and abandonment I experienced with Marcello's death and my grandfather's."

For many years prior to the war, Max and Maria-Luisa had interacted well as a couple because they always found something to do. Beyond those romantic, distant nights in Weimar, however, they spent very little time focused on their relationship. Their feelings, or the shared existence of their beings, did not progress much beyond the convenience of a professional partnership.

Maria-Luisa could feel herself withdraw, pained by yet another loss. She sensed Max took her presence for granted, expecting her to perform a function, not believing the relationship had purpose or connection at a deeper, emotional level.

"I am alone, not truly connected to Max," she confessed to a friend over tea one afternoon while Max was out. "I have accepted a new reality where each plays our role, so we both act the part the other expects or requires. I have shut down, fundamentally locking Max out of my soul."

"Oh, my poor dear," said her friend as she patted her arm.

"I wonder if I was really with him, or just going through the motions, each day into the next, time slipping away, waiting for the roles to play out versus being conscious and purposeful."

Max felt a callousness, an indifference, toward Maria-Luisa as well, in reaction to her distance. Protecting himself, he became resentful of the loss of connection.

"I no longer play the role of savior," he admitted to himself. "My ego ceases to receive support."

His bitterness grew, fueled by the envy he felt. Maria-Luisa projected a sense of strength and independence, not appearing to be phased by the death of her father or any of the other setbacks in her life.

"These things must happen for something better to come along," she told him.

He stalked out, slamming the door behind him.

* * *

In 1943, the Third Reich assigned Strub to preserve original works by German composers. Some of these were stored in archives across German-influenced cities, such as the archives at Kladsko, in the County of Glatz in the Province of Silesia.

Kladsko is a historic Polish town in south-western Poland, in the Klodzko Valley, on the eastern banks of the Neisse River. A predominantly German-speaking people lived in this city for centuries prior to World War II, bolstering Hitler's claim on the geographic region as part of the invasions and nationalist politics of early World War II.

Kladsko is located on the road from Bohemia (within the north and north-eastern portion of the Czech Republic territory) into Poland. The road winds through the Sudetes mountains, a mountain range that stretches in an arc from Dresden in the west, across Bohemia and the lower Silesia area and down to the eastern border of Czech Republic. Together, this is the area called Sudetenland that Hitler invaded in 1938.

Kladsko (also known as Kladzko, as well as Glatz under the Habsburg Monarchy and the Kingdom of Prussia) was a town untouched and far removed from the rest of the world or the war.

* * *

Near the archives and several grocery stores, the

apartment given to Max and Maria-Luisa looked out over a plaza paved with cobblestones in a semi-circular pattern, surrounding a fountain and filled with chairs and umbrellas in warmer days. Their home, at 40 plac Boleslawa Chrobrego, Klodzko, felt comfortable with four bedrooms, tall ceilings, ornate woodwork and plaster finishing touches. The walls had a slightly green tint to them, offset by the gloss white trim. The green did not overpower the room but rather exuded a softening effect under the dim light of the wall sconces and chandelier.

A diagonal crack in the plaster ran along the long wall of the dining room, a testimony to the age of the building and the storied community that Maria-Luisa, Max and Chiara were now part of. Window boxes filled with flowers hung from the sashes of the windows of the apartment.

Chiara received home schooling, mostly from her *kindermädchen*, with some reading or music lessons more forcibly overseen by Maria-Luisa. The food and people of Kladzko were the first real connection Chiara had made, outside of her mother and step-father. Little did she know then she would later describe herself with pride as being Prussian.

The medieval history and importance of the town, its architecture, with its dramatic and storied fort, created a fantastic atmosphere for an imaginative, precocious five-year-old child. Chiara always paused when she crossed the old stone bridge, standing in front of the ornate statues that adorned its gates.

In moments of reflection, when she felt left behind or ignored, or trapped in a life she never intended, Maria-Luisa stopped in at the Roman Catholic church *Wniebowziecia Najswietszej Maryi Panny* (Assumption of the Blessed Virgin Mary), on Ignacego Lukasiewicza. The gothic and baroque styles reminded her of Venice, Rome and Turin, of simpler times, more peaceful times. In its center, the Evangelical church dominated Maria-Luisa's second favorite park and reflection area, Plac Koscielny (Church Square). Trees that lined Church Square cut the summer sun and their leaves turned a breathtaking gold in the autumn.

When she visited the park, Maria-Luisa prayed, mulling over her relationship with Max. She recognized a coziness and comfort in the relationship, a still companionable silence, supported by repetition and familiarity. She tried to understand whether the silence embodied a deeper intimacy or instead represented something pitiful, a palpable hatred towards each other, albeit a hatred that lacked form without the other person being present. Were they attached and free at the same time, self-sufficient, yet bound through consent of this deeper love?

She prayed for wisdom to understand the truth of her relationship, love and marriage. She could not shake the feeling that it lacked sincerity and only fostered fear, more a function of external events and forces than their own purposeful intent.

The dependency on rules, along with resentment

and repression, dominated her thoughts, tainting any perception or hope for freedom, light, joy and sincerity. She found no appearance of any urgency, but rather resignation. They had failed to get to know one another, through a suppression of understanding, empathy or sympathy. They remained deadlocked in the banality of daily routine as a substitute for emotional intimacy or closeness.

"Do we really get pleasure in bed? Do we really love each other?" She posed these questions to herself many times.

Perhaps Maria-Luisa assumed that being married to a good person meant the virtues of devotion and happiness were automatically included. Resentment grew in her own mind and heart by feeling stifled as a result of not devoting herself to a more meaningful, fulfilling end. Being defined as a mother and housewife reminded her of the ONB teaching, with all the negative connotations associated with that time period.

Max appeared absorbed, fulfilled by his work as well as his performance schedule. The monotonous repetition without invention or alteration did not give Maria-Luisa a sense of self-worth.

"It's so... such mediocrity to be merely a housewife and mother," she told her friend. "It dulls me, dilutes my own perception of myself. I aspire to be and do so much more."

"You always have been like that," her friend said.

On occasion, Maria-Luisa accompanied Chiara

and her nanny to the park or the open areas near the old fort, just around the corner from the apartment. The sun was shining and Chiara's squeals as she played with other children rang through the air, but the clouds inside Maria-Luisa's heart and mind remained.

The rest of the world seemed very far away. Yet just a four-hour drive toward the north and east, the Warsaw ghetto erupted in violence as surviving Jews fought back against the German occupation.

The Kladzko oasis protected Maria-Luisa and Max, keeping them insulated from any hint that approximately 400,000 Jews were removed from their homes in Warsaw and exterminated. They did not know that the last few were making their stand that beautiful spring in 1943.

* * *

In Klodzko, the scene spoke of birth and hope, the winter fading but the air crisp, the sun warm and pleasant, spring's flowers slowly emerging in the town gardens. Max, consumed with the archives, sometimes traveled to other areas of Germany to perform, often with the Berlin Philharmonic. Max, Maria-Luisa, the nanny and Chiara lived there in apparent peace until January 1945.

The expansion of Germany during 1935-1940

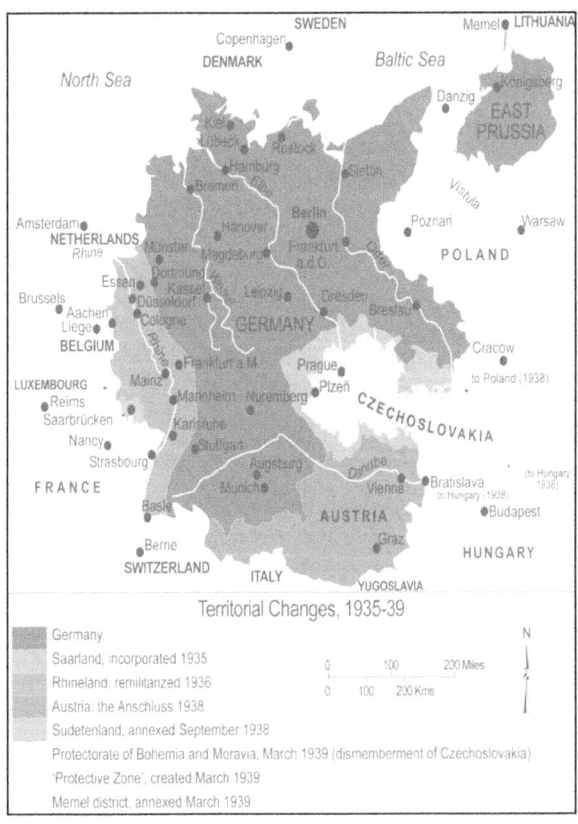

"Territorial Changes, 1935-1939," in Germany and the Second World War, edited by the Research Institute for Military History, Freiburg im Breisgau, Germany. Volume I, *The Build-up of German Aggression*, by Wilhelm Deist, Manfred Messerschmidt, Hans-Erich Volkmann, and Wolfram Wette. Clarendon Press: Oxford, 1990. Accessed online at https://germanhistorydocs.ghi-dc.org/map.cfm?map_id=2884 on July 31, 2022.

Central Germany, Silesia, and Weimar regions of Germany

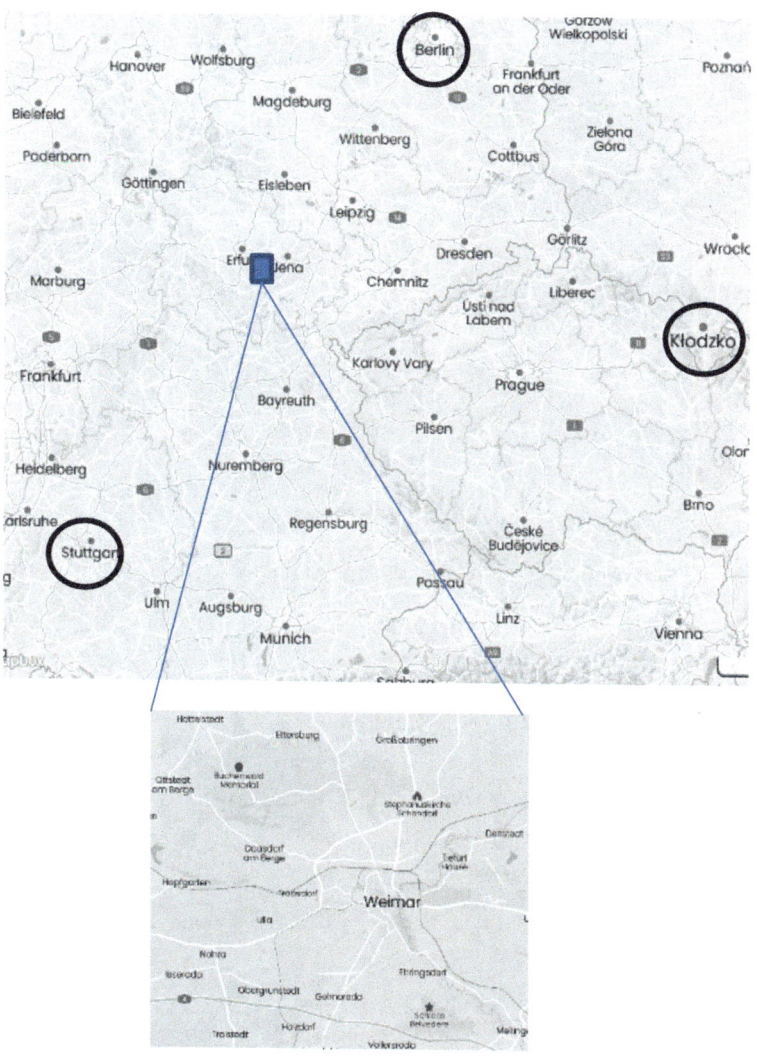

CHAPTER 4

Corri Coniglio, Corri

y 1943, many Italian politicians and bureau-crats fled to Venice to live in abundance with the menagerie of spies, writers, and film stars populating the city. On that part of the Adriatic, life proceeded unaffected by the war, so the parties seemed unceasing. People attended elaborate dinners, drank as much wine as they desired. They gambled with their fortunes. They went to the beach or attended film festivals, football (soccer) tournaments, and the opera at Teatro Malibran. The 1943-44 season program at Teatro la Fenice included *La Boheme, Mefistofele,* and *Madama Butterfly.* Volpi organized music festivals, film festivals, and moonlit concerts in Piazza San Marco. The bordellos recalled the ancient glory days of Naples and Nero, with almost continuous orgies.

In Venice, no one paid attention to the Allies' advancement into Italy, launched in July 1943 in the areas nearby, including Sicily and Naples. With only passing interest, a few revelers watched the Grand

Council depose Mussolini that same month. Outside of Venice, the Italian people were demoralized, while the Council concluded the war had been lost.

Mussolini, arrested after the Council rendered a vote of "no confidence," was imprisoned in the penal settlement on the island of Ponza. King Vittorio Emmanuel III, reinstated as the leader of Italy, assumed a figurehead role without any mandate or direction.

Meanwhile, Venice partied.

* * *

"Max!" Maria-Luisa called out as she listened to the news on the radio. "Italy is going *stunad*. It's that King… Emmanuel, he called for an armistice with the Allies on September 8th! But the Germans still occupy Venice plus the regions near there along the Adriatic. I am worried about my friends. Our country is now split in two!"

Max had gathered some of this from the troops stationed in the area. He also was aware they were arresting known leaders such as Volpi and Vittorio Cini, a senator and the Minister of Communications.

Max told Maria-Luisa what he knew, adding, "I think it's going to be okay. Order will return. When they invaded Venice and its surrounding region, they freed Mussolini from prison, setting him up as the head of the Italian Social Republic. It's a new Republican government; maybe his reinstatement and alliance with Hitler will help regain some stability."

"But I hear rumors that Mussolini is confined to an estate on Lake Garda."

"Much like D'Annunzio in his post glory days, yes?"

"I wonder if he will turn out to be merely a puppet for the Führer," Maria-Luisa said with a long sigh.

Max frowned at her as he shook his head.

Maria-Luisa kept abreast of the emerging news, following the turn of events. With Mussolini's release, the King feared for his life, as well as for his family's, so he soon fled Rome, abdicating the throne to the crown prince Umberto.

"I don't see any signs of stability, Max," Maria-Luisa wailed. "It's all chaos. They say the King is hiding in an Allied-controlled town on the Adriatic, rumored to be Brindisi. I hear the Nazis have incarcerated his daughter, Mafalda!"

"But there is something else, Max," Maria-Luisa whispered in a tense tone, strained by the thought of it. "My family tells me of several thousand Jews that Mussolini claimed to have deported were instead sent to German prison camps and never heard from again. Plus, rumors are going around that people are being killed in gas chambers at these prison camps." Her hands clenched into fists, her eyebrows raised, hoping these reports could not be true.

"I know these young men, these soldiers. Think of that group of officers we made friends with all those summers in Weimar. Do you really see them as capable of such things?" Max said in a terse tone. "I doubt what you are hearing is true. It sounds more like Allied forces propaganda to me, not news or truth."

Maria-Luisa listened to Max with a hopeful eagerness, a willingness to discredit the stories. Communication had become more difficult as 1943 gave way to 1944. She lost touch with her friends in Venice and Monterubbiano. Listening to the unfolding stories of strange happenings, she wondered if Klodzko would also experience the same turmoil, to find their lives upended the same way.

In November 1943, Maria-Luisa received a letter from one of her relatives in Turin.

"Max," she called out, "Listen to this! My Aunt Josephine in Turin describes an Italy split in half, divided by two opposing military forces with Italians fighting alongside the Germans against other Italians who are fighting alongside the Allies! This is so sad," she continued, "because it appears to go from Salerno to the Po Valley. It's the whole country!" she sobbed.

Max raised his head from the score he was studying. "Did she say anything about Venice? Any word on how other cities like Rome or Milan are faring? I was supposed to be performing there in a few months."

Maria-Luisa jumped to her feet and left the room, slamming the door behind her.

A few months later, Max received notice about his Venice performances.

"Well, Maria-Luisa," he said, "it appears matters are worse than what I had hoped for. My performance in Venice was canceled."

"Why?" she said, only half listening to the prattle, stirring her coffee, watching the swirls of steam rise from the cup and vanish the way so many of her own career aspirations had gone. How cruel of him, she thought. He should go to Venice anyway. She held back the smirk the idea brought her.

"Evidently anti-fascist protestors have been storming the stages at Venetian theaters, attacking the wealthy... encouraging people to rise up and join the resistance." Max paused again, running his fingers through his hair. "This is hysteria, this reaction, its nothing more than hysteria. These protestors are seizing a moment, not defining a bona fide political movement!"

Maria-Luisa paced as she followed the events to the extent they were reported on the radio. After an hour of listening, she reached over and flipped the dial to 'off'. "It seems everything is falling apart," she cried.

Maria-Luisa's premonition that September of 1944 came true just a few months later.

* * *

In her apartment in Klodzco, Maria-Luisa sat at the piano provided for them, practicing one of her favorite pieces, Brahms *Piano Concerto No. 2.* Max watched from the kitchen as with great intensity she approached the conclusion of the second movement, her furious fingers pushing the keys, her head and body lifting, then dropping in motion with her forearms, emphasizing the fury of the movement's passionate, bombastic conclusion.

To the north, that same October in 1944, Russia's Red Army initiated a massive offensive against German forces guarding the eastern front of German-occupied territories. The attack stretched from the Baltic Sea almost to the Adriatic. The East Prussia offensive, as it was later called, included over 1.5 million soldiers combined with Russian and Czech forces, whose sole purpose was aimed at crushing the nearly 700,000 German soldiers occupying Russia, Poland, Hungary, Czechoslovakia and Yugoslavia.

Five hundred miles from where Maria-Luisa concluded that stormy second piano movement, the two-pronged assault was launched in the north, with bombardments and a massive heavy artillery push along the coast of the Baltic Sea and northern Poland. The southern prong of the strike intended to divide German resources as Russian troops pressed along the Elbe River into Austria and Czechoslovakia. Fighting was as frenzied as Maria-Luisa's playing of Brahms' concerto.

* * *

Maria-Luisa and Max crowded together next to the radio, listening to the emerging news of the Russian onslaught on the German town of Nemmersdorf (now known as the Russian town of Mayakovskoye). News reports criticized the Russians for using tanks to bulldoze through the simple town, crushing carts filled with belongings of people fleeing, in many cases crushing the people as well.

Maria-Luisa shook with terror at the reports of infantry trucks disgorging soldiers who rampaged through the town, raping villagers and pillaging. "Max," she said, gasping as she grabbed his arm, "talk to the guards to find out if this is true. I need to know if we are in danger. We cannot travel fast if we need to, with Chiara plus a nanny to consider."

After discussing with the commander of the troops in town, Max returned home the following day. "Maria-Luisa, they told me this viciousness is being repeated all along the Eastern front. The Red Army is raping, looting and killing anything German. We need to make plans to leave if the situation gets worse. We will be safer farther west, closer to Dresden and Berlin."

"I just don't know what we should do right now," she said. "I am doubting the stories about the Russians. I am beginning to believe we are being manipulated. But why would the Third Reich lie to distort things?"

"Indeed, what would be the point of that?" said Max. "Do you think they want us to join the fight, that somehow our contribution will make the difference in the resistance to the Russian attack?"

"I don't know!" screamed Maria-Luisa, fuming, channeling her frustration and anxiety at Max. "The radio accounts of the Red Army atrocities make me afraid. I saw a caravan of people of German-speaking people already moving west through town yesterday. If there's going to be a massive migration out of Poland westward, should we wait? I want to avoid the Russians. I'd be more comfortable leaving sooner, without having any interaction with them."

"Perhaps you're right," said Max, nodding. "I'll ask the local commander about what plans are being put together for evacuation."

Max didn't mention he knew about special accommodations established for members of the Fuhrer's list.

* * *

No one at the time imagined that actions of the Red Army may have been purposeful retribution, vengeance for the Nazi brutality during the German invasion in Russia and Moscow a few years earlier in 1941-1942.

The winter of 1944-1945 raged bitter and harsh across Europe. Max and Maria-Luisa struggled to stockpile enough gas and firewood to keep the house warm and Chiara healthy.

Between the wicked weather and intense German resistance, the Russians achieved minimal progress with the initial 1944 effort. An uneasy calm filled the air, yet enough of a respite that Maria-Luisa pined to practice certain movements from Chopin.

She found solace in the second movement of his *Piano Concerto No. 1*. The light, airy required keystrokes, the softness and lyrical romanticism of the composition appealed to her quest for peace. calming her anxiety. Chiara loved Chopin, sitting on the bench while her mother played.

"You know, it is somewhat ironic, my Chiara, that we find Chopin in our heart at this time. He also had to flee Poland because of turmoil shortly after he wrote this so long ago."

Chiara, mesmerized by the way her mother teased the moments out of the keys, looked up at her mother with sad eyes.

"Enough of this melancholy," Maria-Luisa said, as she switched to the third movement of the concerto which had a livelier, danceable joy to it.

Chiara jumped off the bench and danced around the apartment, bringing a small smile to Maria-Luisa's lips. The smile, the peace of that December 1944, abruptly changed within the first two weeks of January 1945.

* * *

As 1945 began, Russian General Chernyakhovsky, along with General Rokossovsky, mounted an attack on the strategic port of Koninsberg, defeating the German forces. This opened a significant gateway along the coast and northern Poland for additional Russian incursions.

A few weeks later, several hundred miles to the south, in the upper Silesia portion of Poland, the Russian Generals Konev and Zhukov pushed forward, dividing the Nazi forces led by General Himmler. Himmler and his troops blocked the path to Warsaw and beyond that, Berlin. The Russians pierced through the defensive line on Himmler's right flank, forcing him to retreat north and east to protect the path to Berlin.

In that same offensive, Konev and Zhukov also broke the left flank of Nazi Field Commander Ferdinand Schorner. Schorner retreated to the south, into Austria and the Lower Silesia region in and around Prague. Now that Schorner and Himmler were divided, Zhukov and Konev pushed west toward the Oder River and onward toward Berlin.

With Schorner in retreat, Russian General Konev overtook Auschwitz in mid-January of 1945. Prior to the arrival of the Russians, SS officers attempted to destroy evidence of the experiments that had been performed there. They burned hair samples, shoes, and clothes. They tried to destroy the furnaces that gave validity to the rumors of mass exterminations. Regardless of the SS officers' efforts, Konev and his troops found the remnants of the furnaces, tooth-brushes, shoes, and mass graves. Though many remained in disbelief, the world received the first visual confirmation of what happened at the Nazi prison camps.

On Wednesday January 17, 1945, the Nazi defense of Warsaw fell to the advancing Soviet army. Although Warsaw is 250 miles away, in Klodzko the bombardment sounded like thunder, where the ground vibrated from the assault.

* * *

"As I expected, given our status," Max told Maria-Luisa, "special arrangements have been prepared for us. We have a protection detail assigned to help us."

"Who? How will they protect us?"

"A few guards will be on motorcycles, plus an armored Mercedes will escort us to a safe place." He put both hands on her shoulder to try to calm her.

"Where are we going? Do we pack anything?" Her forceful anxiety underscored the reality that this was happening and not just some irrational fear. She twisted away from him and stared out the window into the distance. "When are we leaving? Are the Russians really that close?"

Max paused to take a deep breath. Gazing at Maria-Luisa, along with the nanny holding Chiara on her lap, he spoke with a calm voice when he repeated what he had been told by the local guards.

"The front lines of the Prussian offensive are coming here, the Russians are just to the north, east and south of Kladzko. We need to leave right away. There is very little time to pack. Grab what you can carry. We leave early tomorrow morning."

The following morning, in the last week of January, under the silence of the pre-dawn morning, they left Kladzko, heading west about three hours towards Bysice, now part of the Czech Republic. They were given suites at Chateau Liblice, a resort in the rural area north of Prague near a wildlife preserve prized for its rich game and hunting.

"Max!" Maria-Luisa sang out, "everyone seems to be here!"

As she scanned the lobby she spotted musicians, philosophers, scientists and dignitaries she recognized from their various parties during the summer in Weimar. This was the Gottbegnadeten list ("Führerliste"), national treasures who were being protected from the imposing Red Army threat. The dignitaries and artists in residence there included other members of Strub's quartet. Pacing, they whispered among themselves about the news regarding prisoner camps and the associated atrocities. A creeping darkness hung over them.

* * *

The Russian army crossed the eastern shores of the Niesse River. In northern Germany, they broke across the border, just south of the city of Berlin. In addition to the logistical challenges of moving a tank-based army through the Sudetes mountains, the continuing harsh winter conditions hampered their push to the west. Stalin redeployed Konev to move along the Elbe, pressing onward toward Berlin from the south while Zhukov continued his assault from the west, joining the left flank of Rokossovsky, who attacked from the north.

Meanwhile, American troops led Allied forces to push east from France as well as north from Italy. By February 1945, German gains from offensives since 1938 were erased.

* * *

"Hush! Shut up, everyone! I am trying to hear this," one of the artists at the Chateau called out. He leaned forward on his leather chair, curling his torso over the arm to be closer to the radio. "It's about Buda and Pest," he said in a lower voice.

Others gathered around him near the radio, jockeying for position. Their afternoon cocktails clinked ice against glass, adding texture and color to their hurried shuffles and deep-toned murmurs.

"What are they saying?"

"What happened?"

"Is it the Russians?

"Yes, listen…"

"Russian generals, Petrov and Malinovsky, have

taken control of the cities." The newscaster's crackled discourse continued, describing the decimation of nearly 70,000 German troops stationed there as well as the villainous atrocities of the Red Army, raping, rampaging and looting Buda.

"What should we do? Should we leave?"

"Where would we go?"

"Anywhere! The Russians are going to break the German defenses!"

"Let us leave now. We can get to Dresden and from there disperse. The trains heading west or south. We disappear."

"Keep massaging your mustache, maybe something more intelligent will fall out of your mouth! Our troops will stop the Russians."

"Mind your tone with me, or…"

Shoving and shouting filled the chamber, voices raised, as the debate morphed into pandemonium. A table was knocked over, a lamp shattered. The sound of crashing porcelain made the surly crowd cease its dispute, both physical and verbal.

They debated the strength of the German forces and the Führer's plans to have the Russians go to war with the American-led Allied forces. Proponents and detractors on all sides left the merits of any plan in tatters.

As they continued to argue their plight, the staff served more food. A distant rumble rolled across the sky. The evening's weather was clear, however. Stars appeared, throbbing and blinking in the darkening heavens.

The Chateau's guests filtered outside to see what they could see, searching not just for the source of the rumble but also for the answer to their debate as well. Maybe the heavens would tell them what the sign would be.

Then, in the distance just to the north, the night sky turned crimson and violet as the fires in Dresden illuminated the clouds of smoke. The source of thunderous rumble they sought was the explosions rocking the city of Dresden. It was February 13, *Fasching Tuesday*, the beginning of Lent and the night that Allied (US and RAF) bombers dropped incendiary bombs on Dresden. It began around ten o'clock and continued for hours. The ground shook all the way to Prague.

"They are bombing Dresden!" The onlookers pointed to the sky, watching the growing pillars of smoke rising into the moonlit sky. "Going west to the trains won't work now. We need a new plan."

"I still think our boys will hold them back. If the Americans arrive first, at least it won't be the Russians."

During that Lenten season, peace and quietude descended on the valley and surrounding areas of Sudetenland. Chateau Liblice inhabitants settled into a routine. No one celebrated Easter or emphasized it as a spiritual moment.

Hitler and Himmler executed a programmatic substitution of Nazism instead of Christianity. They replaced Bibles with *Mein Kampf*. Hitler, like

Mussolini, mimicked Nietzschean concepts, criticizing Christianity as undermining society through fear and guilt. He preferred to encourage people to be strong and live life, a virility that Nazism promoted.

* * *

Fighting continued to rage to the north of the Chateau, on the other side of the Sudetes mountains as well as far to the south in Austria and Vienna. Schorner felt the growing threat to his southern flank as Russian troops pounded away and trudged over the rugged hills to the south and east of his position.

In early April, to the west, U.S. Generals Patton and Eisenhower discovered the Merkers salt mine, with billions in gold, cash and art that the SS had hidden. They also came across the Buchenwald concentration camp, finding the remains of thousands who had perished there, as their armies swept east toward Weimar. The Allies pushed hard in that direction, also hurtling north from Italy as well; at the same time the Russians pushed west and south. Germany had been cut in half.

On April 17, two of Konev's tank battalions broke through Nazi Commander Busse's right flank (and part of the break in Schorner's left flank) just south of Frankfurt. Busse believed Konev's next move would be to proceed with an advance on Berlin from the south while Zhukov came from the west.

Hitler, however, was not convinced Berlin would

ever be the subject of a major invasion. He accepted Bismark's statement, that whomever controlled Prague controlled "Mittleeuropa," therefore he wanted Busse to double back to support Schorner near Prague. War records later revealed that Stalin did, in fact, want to attack Prague, but Zhukov, along with the other Russian generals, overruled him by insisting they target Berlin.

* * *

On Monday, April 20, 1945, Adolf Hitler cele-brated his fifty-sixth birthday. A party at the Chateau commemorated the day, including a small hunting party in the nearby woodlands. The Strub quartet played for Schorner and the Third Reich officers, who also took the opportunity to have a strategy meeting on how to manipulate the defense against the East Prussia campaign to coincide with the encroaching U.S.-led Allied forces.

Hitler, from his bunker in Berlin, thanked the revelers for their service and their cheers on his birthday. He also gave a speech of renewal and resurgence to inspire the fight. He reinforced his perspective that Allied and Russian forces will clash, crushing each other, so that Germany will rise up to dominate them both.

Just a few days later, on April 23, the first contact between U.S. ground troops and Russian troops occurred at Mittweida (just west of Dresden). On the

26th near the Mulde River some conflicts did erupt. The report reached Hitler, keeping his theory alive that war would break out between the Bolsheviks and the Anglo-Saxons at any minute.

On April 29, Russian forces closed in on the Berlin bunkers where Hitler and the Third Reich high command were hiding. Göring, his wife, his daughter, and their butler managed to escape to their castle in Mauterndorf, Austria. On this same day, Russian forces liberated the city of Neubrandenburg and the prisoner camp there.

On April 30 at 9:30 p.m., Grossadmiral Karl Donitz, now in charge of the German government, gave a formal announcement on Hamburg radio that Hitler was dead.

* * *

The news reports of the attack on Berlin and Hitler's death swept through the Chateau. Panic of the impending fall of Germany and the possibility of Russian atrocities gripped them all.

One of the violinists ran from the dining hall, screaming, "Run! Get out!"

Uncertain, confused, some sat still, sobbing, but Maria-Luisa reacted with impulsive urgency. "Let's go! Now!"

She grabbed Chiara's' hand, moving toward the door. The nanny followed close.

"My Stratovarius! I will not leave without it!" Max yelled.

"We will meet you at the car," Maria-Luisa called over her shoulder, "but hurry!"

Max dodged through the crowd, sliding to the left or to the right. He worked his way toward the stairs where people running down almost knocked him back. Max arrived at their room and grabbed his violin, then turned to run down the hall, retracing his steps.

They were waiting in the Benz when he arrived.

"We almost left without you," Maria-Luisa said with a scowl.

"Drive west!" barked Max, "away from the Russians!"

They did not know Konev's troops had already swung south from Berlin and Dresden. As Konev rounded the western edge of the Sudetes mountains, he picked up speed. He pressed the tank battalion hard toward Prague. It was the beginning of the Prague Offensive.

They were on an intercepting course. Max's driver saw the tanks heading toward them and swerved onto a side road. The convoy spotted the Benz's official's flags. A Russian military transport pursued.

"Drive faster! Hurry!"

"Stop crying, Chiara!"

The road became nothing more than a cart path. The winding way slowed the escaping Benz. The transport gained on them. The dark night sky devoured the Benz headlights. Ruts in the road jarred their bones. The driver pressed on.

He accelerated around a corner. The wheels sank in mud. The car lurched to one side. The nanny's head hit the window. Broken glass slashed her. Blood poured down her face and neck.

Chiara screamed.

Max opened his door to run. He slipped and fell in the mud.

The transport lurched up next to them. Russian soldiers raced at them, guns raised, as they barked-commands at them.

Chiara cried. Maria-Luisa shouted obscenities. The soldiers kicked Max as he lay in the mud.

It was May 1, 1945, in the woodland outskirts of Melnik, the Czech Republic. They were now prisoners of war.

* * *

In May 1945, when the Allied troops arrived in Venice, loyalty to the fascist party evaporated like fog under a warm sun. Unlike other cities, the Germans did not destroy Venice as they retreated; they just moved out as the Allies proceeded.

The Venice spectacle resumed. The universal appeal of merged history, beauty and desirability as a tourism site combined to form some sort of talisman, warding off any hint or thought of destroying the city.

* * *

Like Venice, Prague remained almost untouched by the war. Its picturesque castles, churches and bridges—all physical manifestations of centuries of civilizations at peaceful rest and bountiful flourishing in music, theater and arts—survived.

The Prague Offensive lasted five days, from May 6 to May 11. It started with a citizens' revolt by an underground movement to remove Nazi signage, since they expected General Patton to liberate the city at any moment. Inspired by the news of Patton's approaching army, the Vlasovites, a group of anti-communist Russians whom the Germans had captured and trained to fight against the Russians, abandoned the German garrison to join the Czech resistance.

However, Patton received orders not to enter Prague. Eisenhower notified Colonel General Alexei Antonov, Chief of Staff of the Red Army, that U.S. troops were able to advance to the Moldau River and take Prague.

Antonov instead requested that, since the Russians stopped in North Germany when asked, he hoped Eisenhower and Patton would respect his request now to not enter Prague.

On May 7, Konev's tanks, instead of Patton's, approached the city, inducing the Vlasovites to flee, fearing persecution. About half of the 50,000 escaped to the Anglo-Saxon line. The Red Army arrested those remaining, to be tried in the Soviet Union for treason. The German line collapsed. The fall of

Prague and the fighting in Berlin convinced German high command to sign an unconditional surrender.

* * *

The Russian command established a tribunal court and internment camp at Strahov Stadium, near Prague. Soldiers brought Max, Maria-Luisa and Chiara there, holding them in a damp room underground, with a long, narrow window near the ceiling on one side, two army cots and a small table.

The first night of their captivity, Russian soldiers, drunk from the celebration of Germany's defeat, opened their cell door and pulled Maria-Luisa from the cot she shared with Chiara. One soldier knocked Max back as he stood up in protest and held a gun on him while the other soldiers pushed Maria-Luisa between them.

Exhausted, feeling defenseless, she was spun around and forced to bend over the table. One soldier held her torso down by pressing on her shoulder blades. Another one of the soldiers exposed her. They took turns raping her while Max watched, a gun pointed at his temple.

Chiara screamed in terror. Maria-Luis could do no more than sob.

This scene was replayed many times over the next few days. Maria-Luisa feared for her daughter's life if she protested. Max rolled into a ball in the corner, rocking back and forth with his head tucked between his knees.

The trauma redefined the relationship between Max and Maria-Luisa. Although love still existed as they continued to care for each other, those soldiers were never far away in their minds. The trauma created a hesitancy, perhaps even a denial, to be intimate. A new source of anger and resentment arose for each of them.

Why did he do nothing to stop them from attacking me?

Why did she let them do that to her and in front of me, too?

For Maria-Luisa, the pain, suffering and humiliation, along with the duration of that crisis, brought her into contact with something deep inside. In some ways she felt more alive, more genuine, more human, stronger, more capable, closer to her true fiery self. She became more introspective. She saw her path forward with greater clarity. She must reconnect with music in her very being, as her original passion and her only true love.

After a few days of internment passed, the Russians overseeing the tribunal court summoned the family. The military court obtained the Gottbegnadeten list with Strub's name, which to them implied he must be a war criminal as a highly placed member of the Third Reich.

Max argued his status as a valued German asset of musical talent. Soldiers put guns to the foreheads of both Chiara and Maria-Luisa. He was forced to prove his musical profession by an audition.

Chiara watched, frozen, sniffling, unable to cry anymore at this point, the smell of gunpowder from the muzzle of the gun to her face, burning her nose, the heat singeing her cheek, while her father auditioned for their lives. When he finished playing, some of the soldiers became misty-eyed. The Russian tribunal released them, confiscating Max's Stradivarius violin as compensation.

That November, Chiara celebrated her seventh birthday in a small apartment in Eisenberg, just outside of Leipzig, to the east of Weimar. This apartment was the first location Max and Maria-Luisa could find lodging after leaving the internment camp. Germany's economy collapsed, while the migration to the non-Russian-occupied Germany created a scarcity of places to live.

* * *

Grossadmiral Karl Donitz, now in charge of the German government, did not believe the pictures or reports of what happened at Buchenwald and other prisoner camps, a fault not uncommon among the surviving Germans.

"I cannot fathom such atrocities!" he said many times to reporters and other government officials.

As the evidence mounted, it changed his perspective on National Socialism and the abuse of power in a dictatorship, which have had an exceptional impact on the course of German policies and politics ever since.

Similar disenchantment gripped Italy as well. Anti-fascist revenge killings began in mid-1945, claiming thousands more lives, as a retribution for years of political persecution and continuous war, such as those in Ethiopia, Spain and World War II. The peoples' exhaustion and frustration over-shadowed the social and economic gains witnessed in the beginning of the experiment, which provided improved infrastructure, a reduction in infectious diseases such as malaria and revamped factory productivity. Accepted in good faith in the beginning, fascist idealism fed a people eager for better leader-ship who kept the citizens at its heart. "Proletarian and Fascist Italy, stand up!" they chanted, with the expectation for justice, progress and social solidarity.

Now, these same hopeful people lashed out against Mussolini and government abuse of power in the totalitarian state. The disillusionment reflected expectations of Mussolini, who was supposed to be more intelligent, more reasonable, better than the leaders produced from the old electoral system.

* * *

Max, Maria-Luisa, and Chiara followed the throngs of people fleeing the Russian-occupied territories, becoming part of the massive migra-tion from eastern Germany to western Germany. Approximately three-and-a-half million people came from the Sudetenland and Silesia areas, as many as thirteen million in total fled communist rule. As refugees, with open hands and empty stomachs, western German towns were strained to provide shelter, resulting in crowded conditions as multiple generations were forced to live within one apartment. Supply shortages, even water pressure, affected many aspects of their life..

Landlords cracked down on these intruders. One day, Max received a note from the landlord, prohibiting activity past ten p.m., loud instrument playing and flushing of toilets at night.

"What do they expect us to do, whisper… tiptoe about?" Maria-Luisa whined. "It's getting ridiculous. There's already no smoking and we are not permitted to open the windows. It feels like prison!"

"We really cannot say too much," Max said. "I have my job in Salzburg, but the budget is tight and I don't know if it will last. Keep in mind that so many in this town are without a job at all." Max paused, reflecting for a moment. "And I hear that everyone will be hurt by this Marshall Plan that will replace our monetary system with something called a 'Deutche Mark'."

"Is that really going to happen?" Maria-Luisa moaned. "How can they just replace our money?"

"They have no choice. They have to do something to break the back of the black-market profiteering, even if it means people may lose their life savings."

His comments hung heavy in the air. They did now know when, or if, the Marshall Plan would be put into action. All they could do was wait and listen.

In 1947, Yehudi Menuhin returned to Germany to play with the Berlin Philharmonic under the direction of Wilhelm Furtwängler as conductor. While performing with that orchestra, he also took the opportunity to visit with his friends, Max and Maria-Luisa, in Eisenberg.

"Why did you come to Berlin?" Maria-Luisa said as she poured him some tea.

"I see it as an act of reconciliation."

"You are the first Jewish musician to collaborate in the wake of the Holocaust," said Max. "Very generous of you, of course."

"My intent is to reawaken Germany's music along with its spirit."

"A noble effort," said Maria-Luisa.

"Max, where are you working now?" said Menuhin.

"At the end of the war, I found employment in nearby Saltzberg, where I teach at the university."

"Ah, yes, the Internationale Sommerakademie Mozarteum."

In addition to teaching at the university, Max regained the international spotlight. He enjoyed an active schedule, reigniting his pre-war visibility performing Bruckner's Mass No. 3, with Joseph Messner conducting the orchestra at the Salzburg Festival. Max's growing busy schedule corresponded with a new sense of urgency and energy throughout Western Germany. Despite the difficult living conditions, the post-war atmosphere permeated with a desire to rejuvenate post-war Germany.

"I am so grateful… even happy to be working again," Max confided in Maria-Luisa. "Losing my Stradivarius seems like a lifetime ago!"

Maria-Luisa smiled. "I understand exactly what you mean, Max. I feel the keys and the music and it fills my heart, chasing away the sadness, the fears about being safe and secure. Soon we will have enough to hire another nanny for Chiara."

At once, the air thickened with the pungent memory of that evening, as if the mud, splattered blood, growling engines and humid pine were all around them again. In the silence of the mere second that followed, a magic broom seemed to sweep the mental anguish away. With the memory of the prior nanny's violent death sufficiently squelched, as well as all the suffering at the hands of the Russians, they resumed their studies, sipping the coffee in silence.

In between performances, plus with a new nanny tending to Chiara, Max and Maria-Luisa also attempted to repair their war-torn relationship. They enjoyed moments of tenderness and intimacy, stolen between the sheets of music.

Maria-Louisa approached Max in early 1947 as he sat in their small library. "Max, I have something to tell you," she said in an apprehensive tone.

"What is it?" he said, glancing up from the book he was reading.

"Max, I do not know how else to… so I will just say it… I'm pregnant."

Occupation of Germany, 1945

https://www.nato.int/cps/en/natohq/declassified_136311.htm
accessed August 21, 2022

CHAPTER 5

Prospero

Max grabbed her hands. "It's a miracle, don't you think? A blessing for certain, I mean, who would expect a baby at this stage in our lives!"

"We have been though a lot, Max," Maria-Luisa said with a sigh. "How fortunate we've been and to have escaped Prague as well. Maybe you're right." She bit her lip at the memories.

Maria-Luisa found intimacy difficult to endure. Each time reminded her of the physical loss of control, as well as her resentment. And yet, the pregnancy also gave her hope.

Her mother had told her many years ago, "Maria-Luisa, marriages work because you find love in the little things, in children, an act of kindness, a moment shared here and there, while the rest is tolerated or ignored."

I've tolerated a lot to get to this day, she thought, so maybe a child is exactly what we need.

Eleanora had also reminded her daughter, "Maria-Luisa, you have a strength, a way about you.

You will find your way no matter what life throws at you. You are too stubborn to be set off course by life's ups and downs."

Maria-Luisa recalled hearing this repeated many times, like when a recital did not go as well as her mother expected and she insisted—no, more like had a tantrum—about signing up for the very next one. Unrelenting. Unyielding.

How would this pregnancy affect me? Will I let it? Could the pregnancy give new life to my relationship with Max?

In the days of their younger selves, they had felt love and bliss, appreciating how it all gave way to coping and tolerating. The pregnancy both terrified her and excited her. A newborn provided hope for a new beginning, a baptism, a renewal. It gave her a chance to do something right, to experience a pure unconditional love again.

"The whole thing is surreal," Maria-Luisa told Ney over lunch. "I'm glad you stopped by to see me on your way to Berlin. I feel like I am in a dream sometimes, watching myself go from one scene to the next."

"I'm glad we've maintained our friendship, even if it's been a bit distant," Elly said.

The waiter placed their drinks on the table and moved away. The dimly lit dining room of the Schortental cafe buzzed with a paradoxical vibrancy unbefitting the café's ancient historical atmosphere along with its old-world architecture, complete with hand-hewn beams. The dark, wood-paneled ceilings, wide-planked floors and brick walls evoked a time and place that seemed out of touch with both the more modern aesthetic and the recent desire to put the past behind.

Yet the patrons, young and old, reveled in the warmth those wood beams imparted, perhaps hypnotized by the blaze and crackle of the fireplace. The mystical power of the concoction brewed from nostalgia and fairy tales mixed with the strong Bavarian ale served to please hearts, souls and stomachs alike.

"What are you feeling as you float about in your dream?" Ney squirmed as she lowered her eyes when some patrons at a nearby table pointed at her, whispering to themselves.

"That's just it," Maria-Luisa said. "I feel detached as I float, the conversations... the situations have no meaning for me." She glanced across the aisle at the other diners, as several in the café also turned toward their table.

"Then perhaps this is not exactly what you think it will be for you," Ney said in a grim tone. "I am facing tremendous scrutiny, as you must know. The postwar anti-Nazi persecution follows me everywhere. My old performances when I quoted 'him' during standing ovations are now recounted as evidence as to my guilt and association. The bans have crippled me. I cannot step on a stage anywhere. I am being warned I must recant everything, yet I do not believe I was doing anything wrong. But history is both judge and jury, so because others also did these things, I am now being forced me to rethink everything I believed was right."

"Yes," Maria-Luisa said as she nodded, her voice drifting lower, "I suppose it is now a time for us all to reconsider our lives. I do hope your stopover in Berlin will help resolve these persecution issues for you, Elly. You have always been a good friend to me. I'm sorry it has all come to this for you."

"And I hope you find your peace, Maria-Luisa. You've always had a tormented road."

As Maria-Luisa finished her beef roulade of red cabbage and Silesian dumplings, Elly also dabbed the last bit of the sauce from her fresh trout, straight from the River Ilm. "Now, as you can sense perhaps, I believe my welcome here is waning. I hope we can play piano together again some future day."

In her last weeks of the pregnancy, Maria-Luisa was confined to an Eisenberg hospital bed with respiratory distress and pneumonia. A priest administered last rites. Despite the illness, or perhaps because of it, Maria-Luisa summoned a determination to survive, as she had done many times before. Patrick Strub was born in 1947.

In 1947, Max left the Internationale Sommerakademie Mozarteum in Salzburg to take over the master classes for violin, interpretation and chamber music at the Hochschule für Musik in Detmold. He taught there for the next ten years, in addition to maintaining an active performance schedule.

Keeping busy with performances as well as teaching gave Max the opportunity to avoid his emotions that Maria-Luisa triggered. Ashamed, disgusted and at other times, remorseful, Max struggled to reconcile with his lack of action during the internment. He accepted the attention of nurturing, welcoming, joyful women who soothed his troubled heart.

"Wilhelm, I tell you it's an inspiration," he said, "a breath of fresh air, it makes me feel alive, even desired."

"Sure, Max, you are getting a lot of attention that does something for you, which applause or ovations cannot. I can see how rejuvenated you seem with these external validations. These softer, more feminine, more affectionate, more motherly lovers, though, cannot fill your void, Max." Wilhelm paused to gauge Max's reactions. "You will need to figure out a way to forgive yourself or this meaningless madness will just continue."

"Don't get me wrong, Wilhelm, I am very grateful for this life and I love Patrick so completely, he gives me so much joy. I just don't why I end up feeling empty, an incompleteness. I need more but don't know what it is."

"Max, I realize you struggle to communicate what is in your heart, what you really need," Wilhelm said. "Have you talked with Maria-Luisa? You think she has been distant or cool, but you have to break through to her, even though you feel she is unapproachable."

"I have tried," Max sighed, dropping his head. "But it is difficult, tiring. It's so much easier to be soothed, to feel validated by these willing and eager younger women."

"Do you remember your Homer?" Wilhelm said in a sterner tone. "In the Odyssey, I believe the character Mentor says something like, 'He who has not felt his weakness and the violence of his passions is not yet wise; for he does not yet understand himself and does not know how to distrust himself.' That describes you, Max. I hope you find the wisdom plus the strength to fight the self-incriminations, so you can manage yourself better. Seriously, Max you must demonstrate some compassion for what she has gone through."

"I'll have to take your word for it, Wilhelm. It's been many years since I read Homer," Max said with a nervous chuckle as his tone faded.

Max's mind was already drifting away from the meaning of Wilhelm's words. He did not feel close to Maria-Luisa on an emotional plane, bristling a bit at the suggestion he lacked compassion, but where was the compassion for him and what he had to endure?

"Look, Wilhelm," Max said, sitting up straight after his pensive pause, "sure, I want to feel our togetherness again, to feel joy being home. We seem so far away from each other at times... I just don't know where to start."

Wilhelm studied Max's face, nodding, "Well, Max, like appreciating the spring buds after surviving a hard, cold winter, I believe you'll only survive the sacrifice and pain and chill of winter by putting forth some sort of attempt. Otherwise, you will not see spring or the amelioration of your suffering and pain. The way spring follows winter, you cannot attain the joy or fulfillment without the anxiety-inducing conversation. If you don't try, you'll never again know that feeling, or what it meant to come home."

Max turned red, half embarrassed, half enraged by the challenge Wilhelm posed to him. He just wanted it to be easy. He just wanted it now. And he was tired of feeling this lost in-between nothingness.

"Okay, Wilhelm, enough! I will look for the right time and opportunity to overcome the winter."

Maria-Luisa's life, however, entered a new phase of growth and independence that began with a new friendship with a young opera singer named Maria Callas. With a nanny to watch over Chiara and Patrick, Maria-Luisa delved into her relationship with this performer. The near-death experience while giving birth to Patrick reminded Maria-Luisa of her true passion and her own sense of fulfillment with music and the piano.

"I feel so desperate to regain that existence," she whispered to herself.

As a result, Max's tentative outreach found Maria-Luisa resolved to focus on musical perfection to an exclusive degree.

In 1947, Maria Callas' performance of Gioconda at the Arena de Verona captivated a wealthy businessman, Giovanni Battista Meneghini. From that performance forward, Meneghini used his enormous fortune and connections to sponsor and promote Callas. A romantic, he also pursued her. They were married in 1949.

During 1949, Maria-Luisa performed in the orchestra for *I Puritani* at Teatro la Fenice in Venice, conducted by Tullio Serafin, with whom she had performed with many times at Teatro Reale in Rome. Margherita Carosio, singing the role of Elvira, became ill, forcing Serafin to look for a replacement. By coincidence, Callas was scheduled to sing Brünnhilde in *Die Walküre* at the Teatro la Fenice around the same time and was already in town for rehearsals.

Meneghini approached Serafin, convincing him to invite Callas to audition for the role. Callas had not sung this part before, but her sight-reading skills were excellent. She impressed Serafin, but he wanted her approach and delivery to be refined. Serafin assigned Maria-Louisa to prepare Callas for the production and role.

I Puritani was a tremendous success, much credited for launching Callas' career. During her preparation for that performance, Callas and

Maria-Louisa became close friends, sharing similar unrelenting, demanding personalities, setting tough, rigorous standards for themselves as well as those working with them. They also enjoyed laughing at raunchy jokes.

Maria-Luisa and Callas spent so much time together that Chiara considered Callas as her godmother. Callas exhibited no patience for children, however, insisting the nanny take Patrick away if he fussed, or shooting critical glances at Chiara if she spoke out or interrupted. While Chiara did not think of herself as a child at the age of eleven, Callas was twenty-six. Chiara looked up to her, not insulted by Callas' dismissal of her.

From 1949 and into the 1950s, Maria-Luisa influenced and inspired Callas, encouraging her to move past internal misgivings or hesitations.

"Be compelled in every word, be driven, even purposeful," she said to Callas. "Why are you waiting for a challenge to be seen as great? You are great and need to believe in yourself."

Callas' tone and precision also inspired Maria-Luisa, perhaps seeing a bit of herself in Callas. She knew enough to warn Callas. "Be purposeful, be mindful of how your life flows, like this music, these words you sing. Do not be distracted. You have the power to elevate the soul. Be that!"

Maria-Luisa recognized much of her own youthful potential in Callas and was eager to see Callas realize all that it had to offer.

The collaboration between Callas and Serafin at times included Maria-Luisa, requiring travel to perform with them (and giving the now young teen-ager Chiara the opportunity to entertain numerous male suitors). From 1953 to 1957 Callas and Serafin, along with a cast of regulars such as di Stefano, Gobbi, Zaccaria and Modesti, recorded several highly acclaimed operas, including *I Puritani* (1953, EMI), *Lucia di Lammermoor* (1953, EMI), *Pagliacci* (1954, EMI), *Aida* (1955, EMI), *Rigoletto* (1955, EMI), *Turandot* (1957, EMI), and *Médée* (1957, EMI).

"I met someone," Callas whispered to Maria-Luisa in September 1957. "He has a way about him that intrigues me and scares me at the same time."

Callas told Maria-Luisa of meeting Aristotle Onassis, who invited her to attend a party on his yacht. "It was thrilling to consider, but I declined."

"Will you see him again?" Maria-Luisa's eyebrows shot up. "What about your husband, Giovanni? Was he also invited?"

"Aristotle was gracious when he invited Giovanni as well, but I could sense that will not be his intent next time," Callas said with a mischievous, wry grin.

"How could you tell?"

"By how he looked at me." Her grin widened.

"Is this a way out from under Giovanni then? I realize you have not been happy with him or how he is managing your money."

"Maria-Luisa, you know I have been foolish. At first, I trusted him, but I believe he now has more than half my money because he keeps investing it in things that only have his name on them. Yes, he's been quite helpful, opened many doors for me, but still I think I've been taken advantage of."

"Perhaps Onassis won't be after your money, Maria, but are you sacrificing your craft, your focus and your gift, by flirting with such a suitor? Does he have your career in mind or just on his own pleasure?" Maria-Luisa's comment held a note of caution.

"Oh, you are impossible! You have been trying to make me into what you have wanted for yourself all this time!" Callas' tone erupted like an angry volcano. "Are you any better than my deceiving father or my manipulative, blackmailing mother? Is my perfection something you claim ownership of as well? Do you also lay claim to my fame and fortune?"

Callas stormed out, slamming the door behind her. Soon afterward, Callas divorced Giovanni Meneghini to become Onassis' lover. She remained his lover for the next twenty years, including while Onassis was married to Jacqueline Kennedy, until his death in 1975.

During 1958-1960, Maria-Luisa attempted to reconcile with Callas several times, but the fast-paced international life of parties and drugs created an ever-widening gap between them. Maria-Luisa at first felt betrayed and critical of the decline in Callas' health and stage effectiveness. The strained friendship between Maria-Luisa and Callas forced Maria-Luisa to reflect on Maria's final words that day.

Yes, she had expectations of perfection, why would anyone want to achieve something else? But this is how she thought of herself. Now these unrealistic ideals hurt her and her relationship with Callas, so she could not be of support or comfort but merely watch the decline of her friend from afar.

She stared at herself in the mirror, mouthing, "I promise myself from this day forward to try to appreciate and recognize people for who they are instead of molding them into something I want them to be."

For Chiara, however, this realization came too late, thus doing little to mend the resentful relationship she had endured with her mother.

* * *

As the 1950s approached, Max, Maria-Luisa, Chiara, and Patrick moved from Eisenberg to Stuttgart. The city had maintained a stronger economy along with a more robust art culture. It boasted five symphonies, three opera houses, numerous choirs, chamber ensembles, and theater groups. Home to one of Europe's best ballet companies, Stuttgart's artistic scene was steeped in the classics, with preference for Goethe, Schiller, Lessing, Kleist, and Wagner.

The city is still renowned for its hard work ethic and diligence, as well as its rigidity to rules and roles, as well as privacy. The community is religious and devout and at the same time, fastidious and tidy. 'Rigid' is the common description, a stereotype typified in Western press.

In 1970, Hans Günther Heyme produced Schiller's *Maria Stuart* for the theater in Stuttgart. Heyne cast the play with a more modern twist that put the two royals, who are enemies in the written play, as allies in a feminist cause. The lesbian theme and scenes of women dancing together prompted many of the conservative religious Stuttgart patrons to walk out.

This environment also proved too stifling and confining to a young idealistic and energic Patrick.

Western Germany, especially Stuttgart, roared ahead because of the post-war economic boom (*Wirtschaftswunde*"). When the Korean War began in 1950, it spurred even higher demand for machinery plus equipment, creating an even greater economic boom in Stuttgart. The increased industrial production solved the city's challenge to employ the influx of desperate Russian immigrants. Labor costs were kept down, while profits were robust.

On a cultural level, patience waned for those "tiresome intruders," despite their having lived in the city now for several years. By some accounts, it took over fifteen years before the thousands of "intruders," the Silesian Catholics who settled here after the war, were accepted as residents of the Stuttgart community and the cultures integrated with the people who lived there before the war.

Max and Maria-Luisa believed Stuttgart would be idyllic to raise three-year-old Patrick. Stuttgart, in a valley with forested hills on either side and terraced suburbs cut into the hills, offered a leafy, bucolic setting. Its open spaces evoked a more tranquil and prosperous community life. Even the ducks and swans in the Schlossgarten Lake prospered. Life after the war returned to vibrancy with open-air cafés frequented by strolling students.

They were less certain on how to handle Chiara. Now thirteen, Chiara didn't hesitate to express her independence. Her frequent arguments with Maria-Luisa turned explosive. In one instance, Chiara refused to clean her room. She also refused to do the piano lesson Maria-Luisa tried to teach her.

"I want to practice the music I want to play!"

"I cannot not understand this mentality. Learning piano and, more importantly, music, requires discipline and a rigid, exacting manner. The German composers demand the utmost respect and attention." Enraged, she slammed the keyboard cover down onto Chiara's hands, breaking some fingers in her fury.

As talented as she appeared to be, Chiara was never again able to play the piano after that day.

Outside of his performing life, Max's internal turmoil still consumed him. The truth of the Holocaust had become apparent. His complacent naivete weighed on him, in addition to the trauma he experienced in person. "On top of it all, Wilhelm," he confided in his close friend, "I feel such guilt because I do not have the energy to be a father to a child so late in life."

Wilhelm spoke in a soft consoling voice. "Your three grown and independent children from your first marriage are just fine. How is it you can be such a talented, emotional violinist, but struggle to voice your own emotions?"

Wilhelm's tone turned cautionary. "But watch yourself before you have a second nervous breakdown. I worry for you."

"I know," Max said, rubbing his fingertips in a circle against his temples. "I just get this… this helplessness in the midst of a clouded, dark mind. I cannot separate out my swirling feelings. What I want to say and resolve gets convoluted with the additional layer, another dimension filled with resentment caused by my own cowardice, my inability to break through the distance and indifference between me and Maria-Luisa."

Max had approached Wilhelm for answers, yet knew he did not have any. This was his problem, so he had to find the answers within himself.

At some point, Max's affairs were so numerous and obvious that Maria-Luisa managed not only Max's performance calendar, but his dating calendar as well. Chiara noticed her mother's excellent time management and logistics skills to handle both their calendars, which often included travel from Stuttgart to Munich, Rome, Venice, and Milan.

Max practiced a lot of avoiding. He dodged the conflict within himself, as well as the discord within the relationship with Maria-Luisa. He retained the same inability, the same hesitancy to communicate, while feeling the same loneliness. Max stopped romanticizing their relationship, settling into an acceptance of the reality as the punishment he felt he deserved. He wanted to be strong-willed, proactive and motivated, to change on his own.

Instead, Max waited for a sign. He did not want to admit he had given up on the marriage, the failure and the sadness too much to bear. Avoiding it all, under the guise of protecting Maria-Luisa, he mourned in silence the loss of his dream for what this relationship could have been.

"The mistakes, my errors of the past, are done. Thus they are unchangeable," Maria-Luisa told Callas. "Besides, I am focused on my music and on Patrick. Max and I may have been in love in the past, but it lost no time until it became symbiotic."

Callas shared stories with Maria-Luisa, reminiscing on her own challenging childhood and difficult relationships. "You both got what you want, as I see it. There is a stability to your existence, written in reality, not a storybook. You receive comfort from this, plus companionship. Did you want to turn your trauma with the Russians into some sort of baptism? To awaken this numbed sensation that you confess to me, then try to renew your relationship?"

Maria-Luisa sat without speaking for several moments. "I have built walls around myself, because not only I have blocked these things, but also I've never really allowed myself to be vulnerable."

Callas raised her eyebrows. "As you teach, so should you live! You are suffocating any chance of communication. You are ignoring your own loneliness, so your frustration takes on new form. Your indifference to Max and his affairs is proof of this."

"Oh, let him have his escapes," Maria-Luisa said with a casual wave of her hand. "At least that's tangible and keeps the imperfections in the open, likely the most honest thing we have between us the entire time we have been together!"

Maria-Luisa laughed, then continued. "We have settled into obligation and resentment, neither motivated nor inspired to do anything for each other in this relationship."

"We each understand this is a half-truth," said Maria.

"Finding new love is daunting, especially with children," Maria-Luisa said with a sigh. "I am too hesitant to leave or move forward for myself. I don't need to explore that option."

Both knew these words did not need to be said out loud.

Maria shrugged. "As long as you understand that staying means to pay a personal toll, while leaving requires a different payment."

In 1953, Strub and Maria-Louisa divorced on the eve of Chiara's sixteenth birthday. Maria-Luisa's ambivalent demeanor during the transition reflected her survival instinct.

"I choose to not be bitter, but instead my philosophy is that love is life. As long as there is love, it does not matter what those relations were nor it does matter if relationships come or go."

The year 1953 also witnessed the death of Maria-Luisa's mother. Maria-Luisa reacted to the news with an ambivalence equal to her divorce from Max.

"How can you show such a lack of emotional response?" Chiara cried. "Your distance… your emotional walls… they're appalling."

"You don't understand—"

In all of her resentment fed by teenaged hormonal rage, Chiara wanted to escape this madness so she could experience real love. She wanted the attention she deserved. She watched her mother, her father and her godmother indulge in affairs. She learned to use sex as a tool or a weapon. She learned how to manipulate people with her beauty and charm. She was vivacious and bitchy, a live firecracker.

Some compared her to a pin-up model such as Sophia Loren, with her fiery eyes and luxurious black hair. Chiara flaunted the restrictions of Stuttgart life every turn she could find. She liked to be loud and she liked to dance, to be ostentatious at dinner parties and in front of guests, calling their attention toward her. She was flamboyant and precocious.

Maria-Luisa grew irritated with her outbursts. Patrick, red-faced, always ran away to hide.

* * *

After the war, while the economy in Germany boomed, it also struggled to reconstruct and stabilize its political and cultural identity, with Allied troops occupying the western half (the "German Republic") while Russia took over the eastern half. The impact in Stuttgart of U.S. military presence included the exportation of culture from the United States into German life, including cigarettes, Coca-Cola, jeans, rock-and-roll and Elvis Presley and consumerism.

The materialism, hedonism and loose morals associated with the American military's way of life also manifested in striptease parlors, prostitution, common-law marriages and increasing numbers of illegitimate births.

American general infantrymen (GIs) serving in Germany in the 1950s were morally and emotionally conflicted. On one hand, being stationed in Germany generated a sense of relief – the Korean War draft had landed them in a much safer war zone. The term "tourist soldier" was coined because GIs stationed in Germany attended USO shows, traveled throughout Europe and played sports.

At the same time, many friends from boot camp now served in Korea. Not being stationed in Korea, nor part of the active fight, stirred guilt in some of the soldiers. Many German-based GIs refused their Occupation Service Medal, reasoning that they did not deserve recognition. U.S. government propaganda promoted their role as prevention against the Soviet invasion of West Germany, and further that the German people were grateful for their presence and assistance in rebuilding the country. However, the documented interviews with soldiers after the war indicate they did not share this sentiment or perspective.

Stuttgart became a major staging area for U.S. troops and the U.S.-European Command center during the Cold War. As tensions between the U.S. and Russia flared, U.S. Army VII Corps (the "Jayhawks") were assigned to Hellenen Kaserne (renamed Kelley Barracks in 1951). The U.S. bases around Stuttgart are Patch Barracks, Robinson Barracks, Panzer Kaserne and Kelley Barracks.

From the end of World War II until the early 1990s, numerous forces have been stationed there, though predominantly Army. During the 1940s and 1950s, the Jayhawks, the 1st infantry ("Big Red One") and the Seventh Army were the main forces stationed in Stuttgart. Other forces included the 1st Battalion, the 10th Special Forces Group (that included HQ in Kelley), the 5th Battalion and the 2nd Air Defense Artillery.

Top secret surveillance missions disembarked from Stuttgart. Some of these were shot down or did not return. Tanks and other ordinance, such as anti-aircraft weapons, were used extensively for training exercises in the event of Russian attack.

The constant state of preparedness kept the motor pool and mechanics busy doing field repairs or hauling equipment back to base for more intense repairs. Tanks got stuck in the marshes or the bogs. Frequent alerts sent troops out into the field to patrol the border between East and West Germany. Special training sessions simulated war games. T18 infantry carriers stayed at the ready to provide fast mobilization, complete with mortars and machine guns.

The strain of a busy work schedule, the constant threat of the unknown and uncertain act of aggression and the anti-American resentment, plus threats against military personnel by younger Germans, created a very stressful situation for some. In recorded verbal accounts of the state of stress each soldier confronted, one GI recounted how a member of his squad in boot camp broke under the duress, using a bottle opener to slash at other soldiers sleeping in the same barracks.

Daily life on a Stuttgart base mimicked life in the United States, with shops and sidewalks reminiscent of a small town, Anywhere, USA. Soldiers found schools, grocery stores with American goods, gas stations, pharmacies, chapels and movie theaters. GIs hired German women to clean their homes on the base and wash their laundry. Most saw this opportunity as contributing to the economic opportunities for the Germans who had suffered from the war, while others considered this to be exploitive of their economic plight.

After the war, the number of women was significantly higher than men in Germany, so it fell to the women to find ways to earn a living, even though most were raised under the Nationalist ideals that a woman is not to have a profession but rather tend to all matters of house and home.

In post-war Germany, many German women provided for their families by working on the American military bases as waitresses, bartenders, nurses, housemaids and nannies, but also by being prostitutes. Developing personal relationships with American men meant potential financial security and possibly an exit from Germany.

In many cases, soldiers were not only happy to have fallen in love with the opportunity to marry a "traditional" woman, but they also expressed satisfaction providing American citizenship to their wives, "saving them" from their war-torn and rigid, backward European past. Soldiers who married German women felt their wives "owed them." Most servicemen were dismissive of or looked down on German women who frequented bars or worked as prostitutes. Some soldiers expressed sympathy for the plight of the war survivors but also felt a sense of entitlement. They expected recognition, deference, respect and obeisance from these "traditional" women.

* * *

Chiara grew to be a woman in this environment but lacked a sense of acceptance or belonging.

Her relationship with her mother left her without an emotional anchor or connection. She found herself needing intellectual intercourse as much as emotional bonds. She felt a cultural divide between the old-fashioned ideology of her mother and the new world attitudes, including the permissiveness of the American soldiers. Her deep desires were not being satisfied, resulting in an emptiness and loneliness. She expressed frustration with life in Germany and with her mother.

The traditions, music and food felt stagnant, almost suffocating, compared to that of the Americans. Her growing discontent expanded into a war cry of sorts, an internal maelstrom of energy, seeking inspiration, challenge and opportunity to experience life.

"I want to escape this dead end, to move beyond... to break free from my present circumstance, this awful life," she growled to herself in private.

Without the hope and dream of that, Chiara could only feel the crush of the soulless, spirit-deprived reality that she felt in Stuttgart. Her restlessness combined with her resentment, priming her for destructive behavior. To Chiara, love was a function of trust, but she was only willing to trust love if she could possess it, reign over it. She lost no time in learning she could control men along with their attention with a physical connection. She tore through many relationships, attempting to fill in or compensate for the gaps and omissions, but they were discarded if they did not address her needs.

In 1955, Chiara, now eighteen, worked on the Stuttgart base in its tavern, both as a waitress and a bartender and at the base hospital as a nurse's aide. Unaware of Chiara's nightlife, Maria-Luisa travelled, performing with Callas.

On top of her busy work schedule, Chiara spent her free nights experiencing the vibrant Stuttgart nightlife. As a child, Chiara's home-schooling emphasized the classics, in particular opera. She studied anything Callas performed.

Her interests now extended beyond opera, accompanying the handsome young soldiers who preferred jazz clubs. Her favorite dress featured a sapphire-blue silken top, a boat neckline draped halfway across her shoulders, honeycomb-tessellated black lace extended up to the nape of her neck, leaving enough neckline exposed for her pearl choker.

The black chiffon skirt extended from her thin waist to halfway below her knee. Her high-heeled shoes accentuated her calf muscles and toned legs just enough without being too much for Stuttgart sensibilities, yet somehow were just a bit more, in a Milan-fashionista sensibility. Her dress hugged her waist just tight enough to not disguise her alluring figure, yet not too tight as to prevent her from being able to dance all night.

Her black hair flowed and swayed below her shoulders. The candlelight, even in the haze of cigarette smoke, accentuated her smoldering, fierce eyes. The faint reflection of moisture on her rosy cheeks gave testament to the twirling swirling and racing hearts on or off the dance floor. The upbeat jazz tempo of the quartet on stage completed the hypnotic frenzy that Chiara embodied.

The attention was on her and she loved every ounce of it. Chiara's vivaciousness acted like a flame, flickering and dancing, undulating, and enticing, drawing men toward her like a moth. They could not resist.

Some nights, so many soldiers from the base gathered in the courtyard outside their home, pitching pebbles at Chiara's bedroom window, vying for her attention, that Maria-Luisa called the military police to chase them away. Her stern tone, combined with her disapproval of Chiara's actions, only served to goad Chiara into higher levels of outlandish behavior and acts of rebellion.

During a fall 1955 performance of Beethoven and Mozart symphonies by the Seventh Army Symphony Orchestra, Chiara met Corporal Nathan Damico, 8th Ordinance Company, Seventh Army. He was a tall, dark-haired, dashing trumpet player in the orchestra.

Chiara had noticed him in the tavern a few times. Nathan captured her attention by being polite, yet quiet and intense.

"My family emigrated from Palermo, Sicily, at the turn of the century. They became landlords in New York's Little Italy," he told her.

"Well, you speak Italian in a fluid, smooth cadence, despite being American, though with a definite accent... hmmm."

He put his lips to her ear and whispered, "It probably reflects the combined influence of New York's Mulberry Street and my traditional Sicilian heritage."

They soon discovered they were equals in passionate temperament, physical beauty and sense of adventure.

"I like to leave the base with you on the motorcycle you borrow from the motor pool," she said as she straddled the seat and wrapped her arms around him. "I can let my hair whip in the wind as we drive through the countryside."

Smiling, he turned to put his hand on her cheek, then brushed her long dark hair off her shoulder.

Quite often they went to a field or a lakeside for a picnic. Most times, they just wanted to get away and be together, free and in love.

In January 1956, a torrent of blood streamed down Chiara's leg while she was working at the nurse's station in the base hospital. Chiara had not even realized she was pregnant. When the news reached him, Nathan drove to the hospital as fast as he could from the field maneuvers he participated in with his unit. These maneuvers were part of the coordinated U.S. and European forces preparation for Soviet invasion.

Over the next several weeks, doctors diagnosed the malformed fetus as having Cooley's Anemia, a serious form of thalassemia, a rare hereditary blood disease that affects production of hemoglobin and impairs red blood cell oxygen levels.

"Cooley's Anemia is a particular strain of anemia that is most highly concentrated in Sicilian bloodlines, which both of you share," the doctor told them.

In his office, they sat stiff in their chairs, gripping each other's hand.

Undeterred by their loss, their love ever stronger from the shared experience, Nathan and Chiara once again lost another pregnancy to Cooley's Anemia in the summer of 1956.

The New Year's Eve celebration, January 1957, included a performance on the base by the orchestra, followed by a jazz ensemble and dancing. Champagne flowed, Chiara wore her favorite dress, while Nathan looked sharp as ever in his pressed uniform, starched white shirt and spit-polished shoes.

They partied to say goodbye to a difficult, emotional year, farewell and good riddance! In that moment, they put hopes and dreams front and center, to imagine a life together and clung to each other. Surely 1957 would be a better year. Chiara and Nathan made love that evening with an intensity that bordered on desperation, as well as deep longing.

Outside of the Army base, the shortage of cash provided ideal conditions for the development of a black-market economy. American cigarettes were the preferred form of currency, so GIs converted their cigarette allotment into liquor, cosmetics and other goods not easily obtainable through the military commissary. Cigarettes were incredibly valuable, often sold or traded for considerable profit.

Nathan identified an opportunity to turn a profit. He applied his savvy to develop pipelines of goods and establish trading standards, making a profit on both sides of the transactions. His incredible success allowed him to gift Chiara with exquisite perfumes, fine clothes, shoes from Milan and lavish dinners. They went to the most exclusive, expensive clubs as they planned their future life.

"Remember to meet me for my prenatal doctor's appointment on July 17," she said to Nathan in 1957. "Don't be late."

"I wouldn't miss it for anything." He kissed her cheek. "This seven-month's mark means pregnancy may be successful—"

"Making each of these appointments very important!"

She sat in the waiting room, checking her watch every few minutes. At first, her irritation at his absence soured her mood, reflecting her anxiety along with the uncertainty of the pregnancy after two miscarriages. Her irritation gave way to concern when he did not come home that evening either.

The following day, the base MPs found Nathan's body after his CO reported him missing and potentially AWOL. His throat had been slashed, his pockets rifled, his watch and wallet gone. A supply of cigarettes he would have been selling the previous evening was nowhere in sight.

CHAPTER 6

Tensioni in Aumento

"Do you realize it is almost twenty years to the day that I experienced this exact circumstance!" screamed Maria-Luisa. "How could you be so careless, so child-like!" She paced toward the door, then whirled around. "You are completely irresponsible!"

"Listen, Mom!" Chiara raised her voice to match her mother's, as her face turned flame red as her eyes grew wild with loss and fear. "You can either help me through this situation or leave me alone! I do not need your sanctimonious bullshit!"

The slap across Chiara's face sounded like lightning cracking across the sky. Terrorized, Patrick ran away to hide and muffle the screaming as he had done so many times before during other heated exchanges between the angry women.

"You think I'm happy to have an unwed pregnancy? I loved Nathan! This was not supposed to be like this," Chiara continued, tears now welling in her eyes. "Why can't you understand that?"

She stood in silence for a moment, staring at the floor, then looked up and muttered, "I swear, I do not know how much of your reaction is related to me or is instead a reflection of your own resentment and loss."

Maria-Luisa glared at her, then stomped out of the room.

Chiara gave birth to Patrizia Moresco on August 10th, 1957, an unseasonably warm yet stormy August afternoon. Patrizia was a beautiful baby girl, like her mother and grandmother, with fair skin, dark hair, and ebony brooding and temperamental eye.

* * *

The tension between mother and daughter mirrored what was playing out on the world stage during the summer of 1957 and spring of 1958. The heightened tensions between the Allied and Russian forces required NATO commanders to draw up battle plans and scramble the troops with greater frequency, anticipating Russian invasions along specific routes. High- and mid-ranking officers performed studies to understand the equipment and supply issues necessary to support extended troop deployment and mechanical repair. The management of supply lines and equipment stocks changed often to accommodate new information.

At this time, the Seventh Army Logistics team was deployed to Stuttgart to oversee engineering supplies and equipment. With the logistics support in place, NATO military leadership revised defense plans to extend farther east. Part of the defensive military strategy relied on the Seventh Army, supported by newly trained, battle-ready German divisions under development since 1955. The revised battle plans reflected expectations for a conventional ground war, anticipating Russian troops to attack through mountain passes from the south, east and north. Every day, the soldiers were drilled on war games that assumed Russian forces held the advantage in numbers.

The strategy relied on slowing the advancing Russians with armored calvary and infantry while evacuations took effect. Obstacles were to be erected. Demolitions of key bridges completed. Inflict maximum possible casualties. The 8th Infantry was assigned to the rear to protect the Rhine River crossings, supply depots and airstrips, as well as provide support to the Seventh or to bolster the Jayhawks, who would be fighting along the various lines of defense. The Rhine was considered the last-ditch defensive effort.

In 1956, President Eisenhower expressed the position that the West would not win a war against Russia using conventional means. Atomic weapons would now, therefore, be considered part of the conventional warfare arsenal to be used at the outset of any conflict with Russia, without restriction. With the heightened tensions by 1957, NATO leaders shifted their viewpoints regarding tactical use of atomic weapons as part of their sovereign defense and deterrent to any aggression. U.S. Army leaders ordered exercises and tests to prepare troops for combat where ground warfare supported nuclear initiatives.

Military leaders assumed the U.S. held a clear lead and therefore possessed nuclear superiority. However, in October 1957, the Russians launched a Sputnik satellite into orbit, changing the perception that U.S. rockets could deliver a first strike capability to deter military aggression.

Overnight, distance from the front lines no longer implied safety. NATO leaders were frenzied, doubting the U.S.'s ability or willingness to use its nuclear arsenal to support Europe in a war against Russia. Eisenhower maintained his belief that the threat of the U.S. nuclear stockpile alone would be a deterrent to any aggression against any of the Allies or NATO nations.

The debate continued into 1958. As early as February 1958, a massive war game simulation, involving over 125,000 troops, tested the restructured infantry units, such as the Jayhawks, that were now outfitted with atomic weapons as air support. The simulation allowed U.S. military leaders the opportunity to evaluate the ability to move atomic weapons around a battle theater, with attacks and retreats, acquisition of targets and resupply of the atomic units. The exercises identified several flaws in the organization of the troops and their effectiveness to carry out maneuvers, as well as conflicts between Army and Air Force target prioritization and execution, the former preferring convoys and formations, the latter preferring bridges and rail lines.

Air Force use of atomic weapons also preferred early deployment, with little to no residual support to ground troops. The new mobile force strategy, with its at-the-ready atomic capability, strained military leadership to find the right combinations of equipment, supporting fire power, caliper and nuclear weapons supply and management. Arcane rules and permissions hampered decision making in the field.

The new style of warfare, with emphasis on speed to act and take a position, to arm weapons and deliver a strike and move again, forced the pressured decision-making, normally at the general's desk, down into the field among the junior ranks and section leaders. These soldiers had never been required to shoulder such a burden, thus they were not schooled or trained for it. Enemy line infiltration and reconnaissance training intensified, with the Jayhawks and the 10th Special Forces Group receiving cross-training in demolitions, communications, medical treatment and guerrilla warfare tactics in order to be self-sufficient on extended patrols behind enemy lines.

The strain felt at the leadership level also took a toll on the rank and file. Numerous maneuvers and conflicting orders confused the soldiers, creating anxiety along with stress. Adding to their edginess, scientists published reports about battle-oriented radiation fallout and casualties that was contrary to the advice and guidance published by the Army in cartoon-like information and training booklets. This also added confusion to the soldier's stress. The base in Stuttgart became quiet, on the edge of somber.

After several failed attempts to integrate nuclear weapons into a more mobile, fast-attack infantry, military leaders opted for a different approach. The new strategy relied on fixed nuclear installations.

In the spring of 1959, Nike-Hercules nuclear missiles, which were stationary, silo-ed long range missiles, were deployed in Germany. Construction of silos and bunker installations started in 1958. The first two silos to be completed were near Mainz and Landau. Both sites were chosen to protect Allied supply depots in the area, as well as the major bridges (and evacuation routes) over the Rhine River. Another site near Mainz and a fourth site near Stuttgart were also under construction in 1959.

* * *

On a pleasant spring night in 1958, Major Robert (Bobby) Glennon, Seventh Army Logistics, introduced himself first by his entrance into the base tavern where Chiara served drinks. Fair-skinned, with a boyish, freckled face, his eyes twinkled with a hint of mischief as he burst through the door, already loud, calling out to his friends. He was tall, muscular, charming and raucous, always laughing, the life of the party, ready to pull a prank on his friends at any time.

A high school football star, Glennon, aged twenty, was the middle child of a large well-established Irish family that heralded from Wallingford and New Haven, Connecticut. Never without some of his friends from his unit, Glennon frequented the base tavern to play pool and drink copious amounts with Lieutenant Dan Jurmanovich, a welder by trade, who possessed an almost equal amount of charm and energy.

"Chiara, another round. Pour one for yourself, too!"

"Come dance with us!"

"Chiara, won't you smile for us?"

"Chiara, why do your eyes sparkle with fire?"

"Chiara! Tell the cook he messed up my burger!"

"Chiara! Come with us to the jazz club later!"

The dynamic duo lost no time in integrating the sassy and vivacious Chiara into their nighttime plans.

Bobby did not attempt to mask his interest in Chiara, so their frequent flirtations soon developed into romance. On afternoons when Bobby had no field assignment, they went on romantic picnics or walks at Rosenstein Park in Stuttgart. The park flowed with roses, Chiara's best-loved flower, also the favorite of King Wilhelm I's wife, Queen Catherine, sister to the Russian Tsar Alexander I. The park is their old castle grounds.

The gardens followed the English style of landscape design, with extended grassy areas separating species of trees and plants. The long paths and open spaces were perfect for relaxed strolls or quiet picnics, away from all the stress and anxiety, an oasis from life. After lunch under the magnolia trees, Bobby and Chiara visited the animals at the Wilhelma Zoo (Chiara loved the chimpanzees and the polar bears), or, on rainy days, wandered the museum at the Löwentor (Lions Gate).

Her relationship with Bobby was not always idyllic. While Bobby and Chiara shared an intense love of their own, his jealousy over the love Chiara still retained for Nathan reared up whenever she appeared distracted.

"Why won't you let go?" he growled, challenging her distant eyes and lost gaze. "And another thing, I don't want you encouraging the other guys. You receive all the attention you need from me alone." He grabbed her wrist, shaking her from her daydream. "You hear me!"

"You don't own me, Bobby, I'll do whatever I want!" Chiara shot back. "You can check your jealousy at the door!"

"Don't you disrespect me! You owe me," Bobby screamed at her. "I'm saving you from this hell hole by marrying you! You will obey me!" Bobby jabbed his forefinger against her sternum.

Chiara knew a life in war-torn Germany would be difficult, but that did not imply she felt indentured to Bobby. He irritated her as much as she loved him. And they infuriated each other.

"You are so lucky to have me," she said, "and you ought to lose that attitude so you can realize what a prize I am! You treat me better... or else."

She reminded him of the presents and lavish attention Nathan gave her, in part to reminisce and otherwise to goad Bobby further. Plates and glassware stood no chance of survival in their house when their passions got the better of them. The shattered glass and porcelain gave testimony to what had been flung against walls or the wood floors.

The culmination of their fights turned into intense, passionate love-making. The violence and roughness of their love made it difficult for the neighbors to know whether the din meant the fighting continued or they were now reconciling.

During these early years of their relationship, Bobby and Chiara built emotional walls to protect themselves from each other. Their conflicts were unable to be resolved without intense anger or retaliation. Yet despite the sting of these exchanges, the fire and passion of their physical love-making always dominated.

In the spring of 1959, Bobby and Chiara were married in the base chapel. Only a few of their closest friends participated in the simple ceremony. Maria-Luisa attended with eighteen-month-old Patrizia in a stroller, with twelve-year-old Patrick watching over her. Max walked Chiara down the aisle.

The marriage to Bobby could not have been better timed. In 1957, German religious conservatives bemoaned how local German populations accepted anti-German ways of life, including sexuality and amoral women (nicknamed "Veronikas"). New laws, social policies and restrictions were proposed to reverse the trend, including broadening the definition of prostitution to include any woman in the presence of an American soldier. How many times would have Chiara been arrested under these rules if she had not gotten married?

Marriage may have helped Chiara escape the morality-driven laws, but she did not shake off her emotional deficits and feelings of abandonment.

"My mother drives me crazy," she said to Bobby. "She never tells me she loves me... she always criticizes me."

"Why do you need her approval for anything? You're your own woman now." He leaned forward, grimacing as he shook his head at her. "Why do you always need approval or her attention? You think I don't see you looking at those other guys, teasing them? What the hell is this all about, Chiara?" Bobby frowned, rubbing his temples. "Don't you realize how much stress I am under already?"

But there was no room for Chiara to understand or empathize with the mounting pressure and anxiety that Bobby felt, the tension and exhaustion from increased pace and frequency of troop exercises, or the fear of nuclear armament and invasion preparations. His unrelenting duties locked horns with the constant demands from Chiara. The explosive fights reverberated throughout the house.

He would not refuse her, though it exhausted him. All fronts surrounded Bobby, pressing in on him. Alcohol eased the pressure along with the frustrations, fears and anxieties.

A few months after they married, Chiara almost bounced as she approached him. "Bobby, I'm pregnant! Isn't it wonderful!"

Bobby stared at Chiara with a volatile mix of surprise, elation, trepidation and frustration. The adrenaline coursed through his veins.

"What?" he said, "How... how could this hap... happen? Why did you let this happen? You already have your hands full trying to keep up with Patrizia."

Patrizia was now an active, energetic three-year-old with her own set of growing demands and mood swings that rivaled even Chiara's.

"How much more do you think I have to give right now? You couldn't wait until we got back to the States?"

"Listen, once your tour of duty ends, we plan to live in America. Why does this change anything? Plus, you have told me more than once how much Patrizia reminds you of my relationship with Nathan. So, now that you have your own child, it should not bother you so much."

At the mention of Nathan, Bobby shifted his stance,

standing up straight to tower over Chiara. "You're right, but it does bother me, because you always throw it back in my face. Do you know how complicated immigration for that child will be, since she is of German citizenship. Plus there's no documented American father? You don't think, sometimes."

Bobby threw his hands up in the air. "Your impetuous nature is infuriating!" He slammed the door hard behind him as he left the apartment.

Maria-Luisa grew concerned for Patrizia's welfare, given the volatile home Chiara shared with Bobby along with the uncertainty of her ability to emigrate to the United States. In February 1960, Maria-Luisa filed a petition in court to assign herself as Patrizia's guardian.

"Mom! What the hell is this?" Chiara confronted her mother with the court summons in her hand.

"Chiara," her mother said, not bothering to look up from the score she studied as she sipped her coffee, "you are unfit to be that girl's mother. You pay no attention to her even though now you have her in a dangerous home. Your life… you are unstable."

"Oh, so you can do so much better? What kind of mother are you? I spent my childhood with a nanny! That's who raised me. All you did was pay the bills while occasionally criticizing or scolding me." Chiara's fury ran deep.

"Regardless of how you interpret your childhood, I will be the one to provide a stable home and supporting family structure to Patrizia, especially now that Patrick, who is twelve, also has a strong relationship with her." Maria-Luisa spoke with resolute determination.

Bobby weighed in, choosing his words with care. "You know, this sounds like a great solution, Chiara. We were facing significant issues with immigration and all that."

"Shut up, Bobby, you've never been interested in even trying." Chiara glared at both of them. "So stupid and jealous!"

On the day of the hearing, Bobby supported Maria-Luisa's retaining custody of Patrizia.

Glennon's tour of duty ended. Their return stateside was delayed until Chiara gave birth to Bobby Glennon, Jr., at the military hospital on May 13, 1960. Shortly afterward, Robert and Chiara, along with their son Bobby, left for the United States. A typographical error on Chiara's immigration forms changed her name to "Clara" from that point forward.

❋ ❋ ❋

To balance her performance schedule with raising her granddaughter, Maria-Luisa hired a nanny to care for Patrizia. This allowed her to continue traveling and performing with Maria Callas. As the 1960s approached, her time with Callas plummeted and the income from performing along with it. Maria-Luisa taught piano to a limited number of students to retain her passion for music and still earn a living wage to raise her family.

One of these students, the writer and concert pianist Käbi Laretei, happened to be the most recent bride of Ingmar Bergman, the Swedish film director known for his soul-searching, philosophic style. Bergman attended their lessons as well, engaging Maria-Luisa in discussions of her life and music philosophies, mesmerized by her perspectives. Her devotion to music as a central theme, as her one true love, her rock, her foundation, fascinated him.

Bergman and Käbi became Maria-Luisa's closest friends, so close that Ingmar insisted they keep an apartment in Stuttgart so they could visit her on a regular basis.

"See 'love'," she once told Bergman, "as the best thing in life, as the innermost meaning of life. Regardless of the people," she said with a shrug, "the pain they bring, there is always love and music."

Maria-Luisa leaned on his shoulder in an effort to cry, channeling her pain and shame, the gut-wrenching disgust and embarrassment from knowing her daughter had watched while the Russians abused her, the impact war had on her life and her relationship with Max, the distance and resentment she harbored against Marcello, but the tears would not come out.

"Käbi," Maria-Luisa whispered, "I feel so powerless. All my frustrations, my fears about Chiara, I am powerless to stop her from re-living my life all over again."

"What do you think she sees in Bobby," Käbi said, "and why does she stay with him?"

"I have no idea. I suppose it's the magnetism... and being sensual and sexual."

"And he was there to pick up the pieces when she lost the other one, the man you said she loved so deeply."

While dealing with Chiara always generated frustrations or a sense of foreboding, Maria-Luisa felt only rays of sunshine and pride when reflecting on her son. His youthful exuberance and emerging skills as a pianist and musician gave her hope.

Maria-Luisa shared birthdays and holidays with Bergman and Käbi. During Patrizia's birthday celebration, they all together blew out the candles, though Patrizia was ambivalent about participating. Her nanny consoled Maria-Luisa this phase would pass, which Maria-Luisa wanted to believe. After all, the nanny spent the most time with her and knew her the best of any of them.

The relationship with Käbi and Ingmar marked a transition point for Maria-Luisa, saddened by the loss of her friendship with Callas as well as the emotional privation she associated with Chiara. She found comfort from sharing her fears and misgivings not only associated with her personal life and family but also especially the concerns she had about the Cold War.

"My conversations with Glennon give a different perspective than the evening news," she confided to

Käbi. "The safety of my children and grandchildren in such a time of nuclear war are now very uncertain."

"Perhaps the additional nuclear weapons deployed by the U.S. in Europe, especially in Italy and Turkey, are meant to give Europe comfort and a sense of safety against the possible invasion of Russia," said Käbi.

"They only trigger deeper concerns as I listen to the all the breaking news of Russian deployment of nuclear weapons in Cuba as a response to the build-up in Europe."

The Cuban missile crisis of October 1962 was the near-realization of her worst fears. Now an active, aware teenager, Patrick shared her distress. Like other anxious members of his generation, he was vocal, protesting both social and political imbalances. The social unrest that followed in 1965 into the 1970s proved equally unsettling for Maria-Luisa.

Maria-Louisa coached Käbi on life as much as she did on the piano during their conversations before and after lessons.

Käbi expressed reservations about how her relationship with Bergman was progressing.

Maria-Luisa was thoughtful for a moment. "Käbi, love has to be felt for all that it is, both good or bad. Do you trust that I know this? How many times have I tried to control or define the love I experienced, or the relationships I have had. No, I see now, it did not matter."

"What do you mean? How could it not matter?"

"It does not matter because, good or bad, it is only meant to be positive. It will be perfection or disappointment. It will be both fulfilling and empty. See your relationship with Ingrid in its totality," she told Käbi, "or the imbalance between your expectation and the reality will be its demise."

Maria-Luisa paused, growing more pensive. "You see, I erred by not opening up, because I did not know how to be vulnerable or express myself. Instead, I harbored resentment, a darkness inside, because I felt lonely, mistreated, ignored."

"Have you gotten past that?"

"Only recently, my dear. I've lost so much of what life offers because I did not know my true self, therefore I definitely did not allow my inner self to shine. For much of my life, I reacted to the circumstances instead."

"You are being too hard on yourself. You have been a survivor, struggling through tremendous, unthinkable circumstances. How could you possibly be purposeful in growing your true passions when so much of life only worked against you, sublimating those very passions?"

"Perhaps you are right, Käbi. Regardless, remember, please, open up... let go," Maria-Luisa said in a lighter tone. "Free yourself in your piano playing and in your life. Shake off these personal prisons, your anxieties. Don't allow yourself to be repressed. Be better than me."

Maria-Luisa sighed and whispered almost as if to

182 - ❋ - The Road to Moresco

herself, "Don't make the same mistakes."

But Maria-Luisa's premonitions about Käbi's relationship with Bergman kept unfolding.

"I'm so frustrated, so confused," Käbi told Maria-Luisa. "Ingmar is wonderful, but at times I feel like he is forcing me into the acting thing, controlling me and my career. Yet he knows I'd rather be a pianist."

"Have you been opening up to him, or do you let him possess you?"

"He has such a strong presence about him," she moaned.

"Is his ego then leading you to be dependent on his control? Or is it your hesitancy to bring conflict?" Maria-Luisa spoke in a firm voice. "Do you want to continue playing this role, trying to meet some set of expectations that you don't know? Why can't you be genuine with him?"

Käbi choked a bit as Maria-Luisa spoke with such bluntness. "Of course, I want a deep love, where we give each other strength and—"

"Yes, yes," snapped Maria-Luisa, "you need a love that gives both the courage to face down fears as well as the safety to allow pain. Have the honesty to feel and accept forgiveness. Protect the freedom for reflection while you find personal balance."

"I don't know if I ever experienced all those in one relationship. You think that's possible?"

"Attack the piano and attack life!" Maria-Luisa tone turned fierce. "Have the courage and strength, resist the urge to retreat."

"I try, but sometimes I just want to shut down and close off, to protect myself."

"And that is precisely when you need to dig deep, be open and expressive," Maria-Luisa said, as she wagged her forefinger at Käbi. "You must find strength in your vulnerability together. It must be shared!"

"I have a hard time imagining such an existence, Maria-Luisa. That is not how I have lived, so now I'm not sure it is who I am."

"Käbi, forget the past. I know that is hard and I struggle to follow my own advice, too. But if we make the present moment the focus, not the past, or allow worries of the future to cloud our mind, we will enjoy today more."

Maria-Luisa rose from her chair and approached the large paned windows overlooking the garden. Sipping her coffee, she continued, "Joy is a difficult thing to hold on to, but so necessary. It is the dramatic aspect of our very being," she mused as she gazed at the blooms amid the greenery, "so Käbi, I want you to have an unapologetic existence to allow yourself to feel joy instead of reproach or judgment or controls with all their limitations."

Käbi stared down at her lap, thoughtful and troubled. She shifted in her seat, not speaking until after a long pause. "That sounds wonderful and free, Maria-Luisa. I realize I hesitate while I wait for praise from others before I feel a sense of accomplishment or fulfillment."

"What prevents you, Käbi, to root yourself in your own inner confidence and take comfort in whatever you do? Ultimately, whatever you do is for you, not someone else."

Käbi grew more pensive as she shrank away from Maria-Luisa.

"If only you would recognize yourself, your own power and talent, you would never be lonely even if alone or feel unrecognized or unappreciated or inadequate ever again."

Maria-Luisa paused and sighed, placing her coffee cup down on the silver tray, then moved toward her piano. "Let me reiterate. To be alive means being open to joy, to have a sense of humor about everything, including yourself. Although I am terrible at this, yet I have to try. So do you. If you want to get your life with Ingmar back to where you can experience a deep loving relationship, then be playful, even joyful within yourself for yourself, not for anyone else. Käbi, you must let go of your anxieties, insecurities and self-consciousness!"

"Do you miss it, Maria-Louisa?" Käbi said. "Do you miss being playful and joyful? You've been through so much trauma…"

Käbi perhaps saw Maria-Luisa for the first time in the light of that afternoon, a hidden glow of the vitality and spirit of her youth, her passion for life and the looming shadow that cast a darkness reflecting on Maria-Luisa's weary face.

"My father used to tell me a story of a man,"

Maria-Luisa said, "who traveled the desert. This man journeyed a long time, so long that he forgot where he came from as well as his destination. Though nearly blind from the blast of heat and sand, he searched for the cool bubbling spring and running water in the forest he remembered from his youth that would ease the calluses on his feet and quench the thirst of his parched throat."

"I assume you are referring to yourself, how desperate you have felt to get back to that spring and revitalize your spirit."

"Käbi, you and Ingmar have provided me with a renewed sense of purpose and love, companionship and hope."

They drank and laughed (though lessons were all stern business). They wrote letters and shared stories. Maria-Luisa showed them pictures of the parties they had attended before the war on the Ilm in Weimar and of her travels and her children as they grew.

Maria-Luisa found solitude and peace in her music only. In music she saw the aesthetic, an ephemeral beauty. It gave her faith. It was her 'Love.' From Ingmar Bergman and Käbi Laterai, she regained a sense of life not just restored, but also renewed.

Against this backdrop of a growing sense of renewal and rebirth, in 1966, Max Strub died of a heart attack. His death gave Maria-Louisa a jolt because it happened without warning. She reflected on so many memories and emotions associated with the loss of not only Max, but of her father and Marcello.

Bergman and Käbi offered their support, volunteering to go with her to the funeral.

At the funeral service, the expressions of tears and love for him from fellow musicians and friends were palpable; it was a very moving ceremony. Funny stories were shared, making the mood never maudlin.

Bergman wrote about Maria-Luisa later in his autobiography. He featured her as a character under the name of Andrea Corelli, who he said had a talent for "vulgar Italian storytelling, …a hearty laugh, [and]…mad, bizarre, obscene and comical stories." Certain characters in his movies were based on the time he spent with her.

Maria-Luisa was there at the birth of Käbi and Bergman's son, Daniel. Upon the announcement of Daniel's birth, she flung open the opera score of *The Magic Flute*. She felt excited to elaborate to Bergman how Mozart, a Catholic, chose a Bach-inspired chorus (a Lutheran) for his message and her message, of how the birth of a child, how love, can bring reconciliation, both within the heart and within one's life. For Maria-Luisa Strub-Moresco, they were all connected.

Maria-Luisa taught other famous, influential students over the years, such as the Japanese pianist Kazuko Nakazawa, who performs internationally and teaches now at the Helios Academy in Germany.

* * *

The second half of the 1960s witnessed social unrest across Germany similar to other parts of the world. In Germany, the tensions rose from a younger generation tired of the continued presence of Nazi party members and sympathizers holding office and controlling university syllabuses. The older generation believed they were patriotic, defending their country from the aggressions of England, as they grew weary from the suffering the bombed-out country had endured.

The older generation remembered, blaming the Versailles Treaty of World War I for the economic impairment of Germany with the reapportionment of Sudetenland, Silesia and other German-speaking territories to other countries. For this older generation, being a Nazi was the thing to be, to be progressive, to exult a national pride and energy. They were fed up with being held accountable.

The younger German generations did not accept having Nazis in positions of power and influence, including half of the nations' 15,000 judges and members of government. This younger generation looked to their parents or grandparents as the guilty ones, which exacerbated the generational divide.

They challenged the elders. "How could anyone not notice the burning of the synagogues, the massive deportations, the missing people?"

And further taunted them, "Sure, there were heroes, but all too often your older generation didn't say or do anything to stop the atrocities!"

They believed their relatives did not stand up or draw attention to the events of that time as they should have.

"Do you not see," the protestors shouted, "all of Germany, with all its people, has been affected collectively and suffers the consequence of six million deaths in prison camps? Do not avoid the question! You cannot sweep everything under the rug!"

Patrick was among those asking these difficult questions, challenging the status-quo, breaking down the repressed mentality of Stuttgart and Germany as a whole.

As if Nature herself felt the swell of human emotion, on November 4, 1966, a massive storm roiled up the Adriatic and washed over the islands and bulwarks of Venice. The tremendous flooding damaged or collapsed the protective city walls, crushing over 7,000 stores and thousands of homes. It leveled the Lido casino and ruined the Excelsior hotel with massive amounts of garbage and mud. Heating oil and salt damaged centuries old art and buildings, churches and palazzi.

In Venice, students at Maria-Luisa's alma mater, Ca'Foscari, staged demonstrations against the elitism of the music and film festival, calling it the "Biennale of the bosses" for its fascist and nationalist content and tone. Artists pulled their works out of the exhibits, while concerts were cancelled. Student protests erupted in Germany as well.

In 1967, Dr. Aquilin Ullrich, an elderly gynecologist living in Stuttgart, went on trial for his role in performing sterilization experiments on Jewish women and for being party to the extermination of prisoners. The heated debate in the courts as to whether or not he should be prosecuted, given his age, outraged students and those sympathizing with their message.

The German student protests were about many things. They vocally opposed the U.S. and its involvement in Vietnam. Intellectual revolt against the outdated, blind textbooks targeted omission of any references to Nazism. Protests attacked capitalism and the need for societal reforms, encouraging more openness and participation, to destroy the very rigid, authoritarian, and hierarchical culture that persisted in German life. Protestors wanted freedom of expression, sexual liberation, and greater rights for women and children.

Outrage and revolts followed the assassination of Rudi Dutschke, the charismatic leader of the populist movement. Rioters protested the potential role a biased press played in inciting his murder in 1968. Literature, music and design all shifted, reflecting the swell in dramatic political ideology which opened the door for the election of a the left-leaning government of Willi Brandt as Foreign Minister and Karl

Schiller as Economic Minister in 1969. This was known as the "Movement of '68."

* * *

The international upheaval and social unrest mirrored the tension inside Maria-Luisa's home. Much like her mother, Chiara, Patrizia had a difficult, tense relationship with Maria-Luisa. Patrizia's fierce intensity and brooding demeanor favored wit and sarcasm above the rigor and strident character of Maria-Luisa, creating clashes at every turn.

Patrizia also had a terse relationship with Chiara, pained by her abandonment and the knowledge Chiara had started a new family in the United States.

In 1973 when she turned sixteen, Patrizia told her grandmother, "I'm moving out. You have aggravated me for the last time. Now I'm determined to find my own way."

"You'll find the opportunities for a young woman are quite different in 1973," Maria-Luisa said, "as compared to the OMB training and restraints I endured in Italy just forty years ago, before the war."

Patrizia jumped to her feet and yelled, "What a typically cold and dispassionate response!"

Maria-Luisa Strub-Moresco and Käbi Laretei

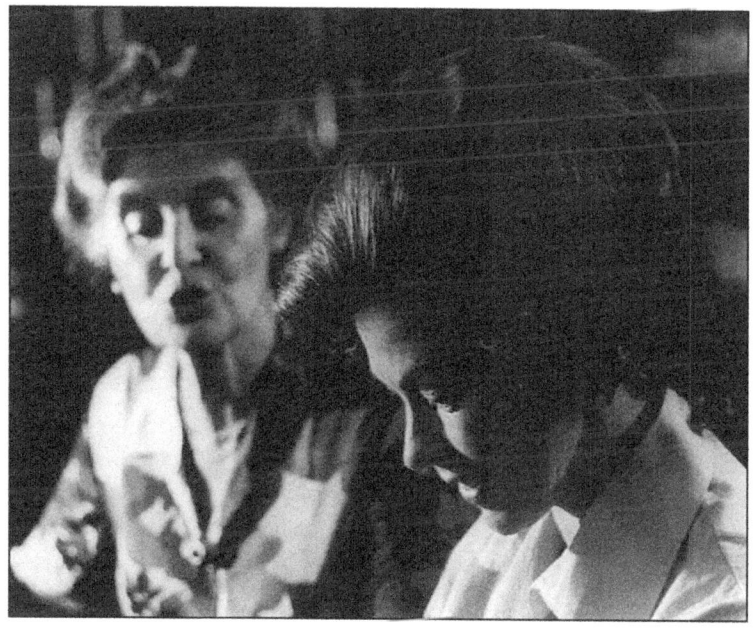

"An Interview with Jüri Reinvere", Accessed on July 17, 2021, https://van-magazine.com/mag/juri-reinvere/

CHAPTER 7

Vivono en America

*C*hiara (now Clara) and Robert returned to the United States after the end of Robert's tour of duty in 1960. To be near Glennon's family, they rented a home in New Haven near Wooster Square Park, where Chapel Street intersected Church Street.

"You're gonna enjoy this bustling Italian neighborhood," he told her, "and we can eat several times a week at the multiple Italian restaurants."

"Cannoli and fresh pasta from the bakeries are always my first choice," Clara said, licking her lips.

"And you'll be getting the best sausage, along with other cuts from the local butchers. The clam pizza at Pepe's on Wooster Street is sure to become your favorite."

Clara found work at Grace-New Haven Hospital (now known as Yale-New Haven Hospital) as a physicians' assistant, leveraging the skills she learned from the hospital at the military base in Stuttgart. Each day she walked past the New Haven Green, where the Yale students studied or played frisbee, strummed guitars and sang quiet songs in their huddled groups dotting the park landscape. The liveliness and energy of the short walk to the intersection of Howard Avenue and Congress Street made her smile.

"It's so refreshing to stretch my legs this way," she murmured to herself. "I like the authenticity and dynamics, such a stark contrast to our monotonous, drab life on that military base."

Robert and Clara's passionate relationship continued, with all of the attending highs and lows, like a rollercoaster, thrilling and terrifying at the same time, full of dramatic twists and turns. A second son, Thymy, born in 1963, amplified the tensions in their home.

"How can you come home drunk every night?" Clara screamed at him. "Don't you understand the duties of a father? Why can't you see how I need help with two children? I can't do everything all by myself."

"Stop putting pressure on me. Quit making demands," he shouted. "I have to cope with the Cubans and this crazy Missile Crisis." He threw his empty beer bottle against the wall.

"Clean that up yourself!" she yelled, then left the room.

"You're just an impenetrable wall of judgment and intensity, a constant barrage of demands and assaults directed at me," he shouted after her. "You always fuel my frustration and anger, like pouring gasoline on hot flames."

Clara returned to the doorway and recounted several interactions that ended in violence. "All your fault," she hissed at him.

Though not diagnosed at the time, it is possible Robert suffered from post-traumatic stress disease. He endured the constant threat of attack and death planted during the frenzied pace of drills in Germany as they prepared for nuclear war with Russia, the East German border just miles away and the silent damage from potential radiation poisoning. Because of a new threat of nuclear war with Russia over Cuban missile placement, intense fears and anxieties, along with bomb shelter drills, compounded his trauma.

The assault continued with crying children and an unsympathetic wife.

"I've felt disrespected, unrecognized, unrewarded... totally unseen," he said through a clenched jaw.

"You drink too much!" she snapped. "Why should I pay any attention to you?"

"Under these circumstances," he said, "even the most resilient person would be vulnerable to the temptations and escape of alcohol."

"You're becoming too irritable, too frustrated by children running around the house with the TV on, making noise. You don't like the way our home is being maintained."

He narrowed his eyes. "You spend so much time

away from home. What the hell are you doing? Who are you seeing?" His voice turned into a growl. "Why do you send so many letters to Dan Jurmanovich?"

In the fall of 1963, this powder keg erupted in a night filled with alcohol, confusion and violence. Robert entertained several friends. They drank to severe excess. Clara was home as well but instead of having any power or control, she found herself in a situation not unlike that of her mother with the Russian soldiers.

The drunken group surrounded her, chanting as they closed in.

"Bobby says you like it rough."

"And you have a sassy mouth."

"Bring her over, boys and hold her, 'cuz I think she's ready!"

One grabbed her dress at the collar and ripped it down her arm, while another seized her from behind and hoisted her up on the kitchen table. He held her down as another man forced her legs open.

"Let's see just how rough and tough you are."

When Clara screamed, her covered her mouth with his hand as he climbed on top of her.

The assault continued until each man had taken his turn. The whole time, Robert stood leaning against the counter, watching, expressionless, while he sipped Scotch straight from the bottle.

The events of that evening numbed Clara for several weeks. Scared, sad, lonely, angry, she looked for respite from it all by listening to opera programs on the radio. On November 22, 1963, Clara sat in her favorite chair, a Queen-Anne high-back floral upholstered chair with ball-and-claw feet, listening to the radio.

She gasped in utter disbelief with a new kind of anxiety as the accounts emerged about the assassination of President Kennedy. Connecticut is a quiet enclave, insulated and isolated from the intense political and social turmoil that rippled through the South.

Only a few months ago, Martin Luther King, Jr., had given his "I Have a Dream" speech on the steps of the Lincoln Memorial, the same steps upon which Marian Anderson gave her iconic performance in 1939. Her concert was held to protest the Daughters of the American Revolution not allowing Anderson, an international opera star, to perform to a racially mixed audience at Constitution Hall in D.C.

Clara felt the heightened antagonism among her neighbors, but she did not fully appreciate how intense it had gotten or had far it would go. She listened to Dr. King's speech and read the news coverage of the marches protesting racial inequality earlier in the year that started in Birmingham, Alabama. She heard the complaints and frustrations associated with differentiated treatment, police brutality and continuous poverty. She did not know the pervasiveness of animosity among southern communities included forcing Black residents to relocate to make way for factories or sports arenas.

The press did not report on the numerous Black protestors who went missing in the South, or were found hung from trees. Nor did the Connecticut press cover the number of times southern police officers arrested Black men to question them about the ownership of their car or to prove they were a resident.

"I cannot comprehend what happened," she wrote to Dan Jurmanovich. "It seems like overnight people now make threatening phone calls to Black residents. Why are intimidating tactics now used to quell voices protesting for change?"

"The same circumstances are playing out across the country," he wrote her back.

"My intuition warns me that violence is imminent, so I'm worried for my children."

She set her pen down and stared out the window for a moment, then resumed writing. "It all feels too familiar, the persecution of friends, the anger between neighbors, the political and social divides that split my German childhood."

Her premonition materialized in 1965 with the first of many riots erupting in Watts, Los Angeles. Riots protesting equality of rights spread across the country to include Detroit, New York, New Jersey and Chicago. Black people felt the social injustices were only compounded by the draft and the Vietnam War. In 1965 Muhammad Ali gave up his boxing title rather than be drafted, refusing to fight "in a white man's war against colored peoples."

The nation's social tensions perfectly reflected the internal turmoil Clara felt. It had the same level of animosity that she levied at her husband.

"I'd like to apologize," Robert murmured one evening, clutching her hand as they sat beside each other on the couch, "for all the..." He swallowed hard.

She sensed he wanted to reassure himself that she is there, will be there, so he could continue to control her. Prior to the rape, when not fighting with each other, they were friendly, almost cordial. She suspected him of searching, trying to latch on, to hold her fast.

She shook loose of his hand and stood up to face him. "Your efforts reek of emptiness and desperation. I feel too much resentment, too much anger to let you back into my heart or even to forgive you."

But why?" he wailed, rising from the couch. "Why can't you forgive me?' I didn't do anything to you that—"

"All your drunken buddies did." Glaring at him, she spit out her words. "The problem is, I don't know which one of them is the father." She patted her stomach below her waistline, then punched him.

Gasping, Robert fell backward and burst into tears.

The pregnancy confounded matters, so leaving Robert now would be problematic. As her midriff's circumference increased, she reflected on her relationship with her mother. The beatings she received for disobeying, for being rebellious and assertive, had built a wall of separation. Her mother resented her, letting a nanny raise her to avoid having to deal with Clara, as well as the inconvenience of a child in general.

Deep inside, Clara did not feel worthy of love. She would take whatever love or attention people were willing to give her. She accepted the "punishment" of being with Robert.

On one hand, she understood and even felt she deserved the treatment she received. She had been disrespectful and mean. She was not accepting, always dissatisfied or restless. She took it out on Robert. She did not have a definition or vision for what "better" would be, though. She found it easier to blame Robert for not meeting her expectations, no matter that those expectations were never set or defined.

On the other hand, Clara wanted to move past being dissatisfied or restless. She wanted to experience joy. She discovered a strong religious bond within her church community that helped her find faith and loosen her desire to control, to search for internal confidence to be bold and allow the next adventure to take shape.

She wanted to regain her sense of dignity, honor and integrity. She struggled to release the anger or bitterness and acquire peace through forgiveness. She prayed that her kindness, desire for love and peace, perseverance, purposefulness and self-discipline would carry her towards greater empathy, generosity of spirit and wisdom. For now, though, she stayed with Robert because the prospect of being abandoned or alone seemed worse.

After Patrizio (Pat) was born in 1964, Clara and Robert first separated and then divorced. During her volatile relationship with Robert, Clara had maintained a casual relationship with Dan Jurmanovich, a friendship started in Stuttgart where he served in the same unit as Glennon.

When Jurmanovich came back from Germany, he returned to Michigan and worked as a pipe fitter and welder at the construction site of a nuclear power plant. One late fall day in 1964, to his shock and surprise, when he came home from work, Clara stood with her three children on his front porch. As they waited for him there, he grinned, then approached the porch.

"My goodness, aren't they all good-looking kids!" He wagged his forefinger at them. "And real cute, too. Now, Bobby is the oldest, right? I hear you are very charming and... uh, funny, too." Climbing the steps, he glanced at Clara, eyebrows raised.

She sighed. "I left him. I couldn't take it anymore."

Dan opened the front door and waved them all inside.

What Dan failed to realize, however, was that the nature of Clara's relationship with her mother and the absence of Strub would forever mold her. She demanded attention and devotion. Even then, she resembled a wicker basket that leaked out whatever love or attention poured into her. The relations with Dan were another fiery and passionate romance.

"You have no choice," he told her. "You gotta stay home alone with three children while I'm at work. That by itself does nothing but stoke your suspicious mind and jealousy."

She scowled at him.

"If you don't receive the right amount of passion, if I come home late, then, in your mind, someone else must be getting my attention. You argue with me non-stop."

By choice, Dan often stayed later to have another round with co-workers or friends rather than go home to that verbal abuse.

One evening just after the 4th of July, 1965, Dan came home to find that Clara moved out. Not only did she leave, but she also packed up everything in his house, including the drapes off the windows. Only one lone empty cardboard box remained, upside down in the middle of the living room, left behind as if to emphasize there had been nothing else to take.

Convinced that Dan had cheated on her, Clara resolved that no one would treat her the way her mother had been treated, or how her mother had treated Max either, for that matter. Plus, in her opinion, Dan did not give her the attention she deserved nor demanded.

The last time Dan heard from Clara, he received a Parental Release form prepared by a court representative. Dan did not know Clara left pregnant, but he was glad to be rid of this volatile woman. He signed the papers without any hesitation.

For Clara, the pregnancy had only become apparent after she returned to New Haven. She rented a second-floor apartment on Spring Street, just off Howard Avenue, a walkable distance to the hospital where she resumed working. In early August 1965, she complained to one of the attending physicians about pain and discomfort in her abdomen. After tests were performed, she discovered two very important things. In addition to her being pregnant, the tests also indicated the presence of ovarian cancer.

Clara's anxiety and fear crushed her spirit. She spent hours praying for guidance and understanding. She cried, seeking consolation with the priest at St. Anthony Church on Washington Street, where Clara attended mass each Sunday, children in tow.

"The challenges of raising three boys as a single mother are already daunting," she sniveled as she sat beside him in a pew after everyone left. "My finances are stretched thin. The uncertainty of what will become of my boys if I don't survive the cancer, or the treatment, terrifies me."

"Yes," the priest said in a calm voice, "the decisions in front of you are certainly overwhelming."

"How can I have this child and still be in its life? Will I be able to be a mother to my three current children? Bobby is so active, now seven years old, doing quite well in first grade. How will this impact them?"

Clara cried at the pain in her chest, the weight on her heart.

The priest comforted her as he could, holding her hand, praying with her. "You might consider giving the child up for adoption. The Children's Community Program on Blake Street is an agency I can recommend."

In January 1966, Clara's oncologist became concerned with the progression of Clara's cancer. She had avoided treatment while pregnant, but too much time now passed and the cancer had grown larger. The physicians made a decision to perform an emergency cesarean section, deliver the baby a month early. They would immediately follow up with a complete hysterectomy, not only to remove Clara's ovaries, but also the cancer.

On February 9, 1966, Clara gave birth to a child she never saw, but who carried her anxiety, her fears and her misgivings. She asked many questions after she woke from her surgeries and beseeched the priest to allow her to see the child and meet the family who adopted it. By the laws of that time, no details were provided to her. She would not know whether a boy or girl, or that the child had intense blue eyes like hers, or that the baby was healthy.

Distraught, defeated, as well as exhausted from the chemotherapy and radiation, Clara found her only refuge in sleep. Church members organized to help her, bringing meals and alternating taking care of her children while she rested and recovered from her treatments. The cancer margins were clean after the surgery.

Clara survived. Most of Clara survived. From that day forward, she always carried a sadness, a heavy, dark weight on her chest, due to the loss of her child.

As if the clouds were not gray enough, Clara learned that Max Strub, the only man she ever knew as a father figure, died from a heart attack. Patrick and Clara had maintained a close relationship, talking on the phone often. Patrick comforted Clara during her struggles with cancer and now she consoled him at the loss of his father.

In those moments, they found time to also discuss and celebrate Patrick's emerging success as a musician. Clara found little solace or comfort in her conversations with Maria-Luisa or Patrizia. Patrizia, aged ten in 1966, understood her mother's sickness, but not the seriousness of it. To Patrizia, it all just seemed like another excuse for her mother to leave her behind in Germany.

Clara's illness and treatments affected each of her three boys in somewhat different ways. Bobby became more stoic, more independent. He sensed Clara's fragility and perhaps her mortality. He withdrew, assuming a more mature stature, more of the man of the house mentality.

Thymy felt cheated and lonely. "I don't like Bobby telling me what to do. Nobody pays any attention to me because Pat cries all the time." He missed his father, failing to understand why he was no longer around. "And why do all three of us boys share one bedroom? We don't have enough space!"

When Thymy and Bobby argued or fought, Pat took refuge at the kitchen table with his sketchpad, drawing to escape the yelling and fighting. The tension of fear and anxiety loomed in the air every day his mother went for treatment.

Clara rested in her bedroom, the thin accordion divider pulled closed, the drapes closed. Naptime was the only period of the day anyone might see Clara bareheaded, after losing her hair to chemotherapy. Clara attempted to maintain her striking, glamorous beauty, often compared to a cross between Sophia Loren and Elizabeth Taylor. She could not allow herself to be seen in public without one of her eight wigs, lined up on her bureau on their Styrofoam bases.

Adamant about maintaining her elegant appearance in the public eye, Clara did not allow for pity. She refused to be seen suffering. Every morning when she could manage it, she got up to go waitress at Al's Diner on Chapel Street.

The owners, Tony and Linda Sacco, were supportive as well as understanding. "We want to help you when we can with shifts that fit your treatment schedule."

As Clara regained her strength when the chemotherapy ended, she resumed a full-time work schedule at Grace New Haven Hospital.

But by July 1967, the city of Detroit exploded.

Black protestors launched an urban rebellion for three days. Eyewitness accounts told of raging fires, looting and terror. Police and National Guardsmen were on patrol, but the riot did not stop in their presence. Burglar alarms rang out of control, unheeded. Drivers of pickup trucks and people on bicycles carried what they could from the stores they broke into. Homes near the stores that were set ablaze also caught on fire.

Although President Lyndon Johnson had signed the Voting Rights Act in 1965, a persistent political and cultural resistance to change still permeated the country. The treatment of Black people had not improved.

In his "Where Do We Go From Here" speech in Atlanta in August 1967, Martin Luther King, Jr., called for an equal persistence and state of dissatisfaction.

"Let us be dissatisfied until the tragic walls that separate the outer city of wealth and comfort from the inner city of poverty and despair shall be crushed by the battering rams of the forces of justice. Let us be dissatisfied until those who live on the outskirts of hope are brought into the metropolis of daily security. Let us be dissatisfied until slums are cast into the junk heaps of history and every family will live in a decent, sanitary home."

His speech concluded with an acknowledgement that the road would be long and difficult, but called for "audacious faith in the future" and belief in a moral universe that "bends toward justice." He prayed that this faith would reward those who devoted themselves to this transformation and they would be able to say "We have overcome."

On Sunday, August 20, 1967, the New Haven Register headlines read:

"Violence Erupts in Hill District"

"Looting Widespread; Firebomb Razes Store"

"Fear and Hostility Walked the Streets"

A white shopkeeper in "The Hill" section of New Haven, where Clara and the boys lived, shot a Puerto Rican assailant. Multiple ethnic groups had moved to that neighborhood not long ago, but their newness also meant increasing tension among the historic Italian and Irish white populations and the newer Hispanic and Black residents.

No significant means of employment in the area were available and transportation options were limited. When the city of New Haven razed several buildings deemed blight and slums, it created a housing shortage in The Hill. The concentration of families needing assistance, mixed with high levels of frustration and desperation, created a powder keg.

These frustrations with living and economic conditions boiled over when the shopkeeper shot his attacker. The riots resulted in looting and fires which escalated in anger when city police and state troopers responded. Firefighters worked around the clock to keep the blazes on Congress Street and Dixwell Avenue under control. The fire ripped through the

Congress Public Market which had served the area for decades.

City officials called in buses to evacuate people to schools and churches in Hamden and North Haven. It lasted four days.

Clara, with her children, lived only a few blocks from the epicenter of the riots.

"I'm warning you all," she said in a stern tone, "we're going to stay inside at home."

"But we have to listen to the shouts... all those awful explosions and to the sirens as they scream by," Bobby wailed.

"I watch the red smoke and fuzzy lights at night, up in the dark sky," moaned Thymy.

Clara shook her head. "It reminds me of the night my parents and I saw the glow on the horizon when the Allies bombed Dresden." Sighing, she held her boys close and waited.

The riots and racial unrest stoked again on April 4, 1968, sparked by the assassination of Martin Luther King in Memphis, Tennessee. Estimates listed over one hundred riots that broke out across the country. Looting, arson and violence rocked cities such as Chicago, D.C. and Baltimore.

She read newspaper reports that the wave of violence did not appear to have as much impact on New York and New Haven, which some attribute to the foresight of those mayors to go into the predominantly Black neighborhoods to express their sorrow and support. In New Haven, some stores closed while protestors initiated a boycott of downtown merchants.

Exhausted, Clara slumped in her chair at the dining table. The chemotherapy, the social unrest, the discord between her children and the persisting stress of having to manage this by herself were taking their toll.

* * *

The social unrest, however, was not exhausted. Anti-war protests heated up, adding to the racial tension. The 1968 Democratic National Convention, along with the likely nomination of Lyndon Johnson, turned into a lightning rod for student discontent over U.S. involvement in Vietnam.

The Tet offensive and its aftermath triggered more widespread anti-war protests on college campuses, with sit-ins and burning of draft notices, which forced Johnson to withdraw from the presidential race. The door opened for Senator Robert Kennedy to fill his spot. The assassination of Kennedy in June 1968 then ceded the opportunity to Hubert Humphrey, Lyndon Johnson's vice president.

The social and political turmoil leading up to the 1968 Democratic National Convention mirrored each other, with all the same elements of tension and expectation for discord and unrest. Eight people, "the Chicago 8," led by Black Panther leader Bobby Seale, were arrested for conspiring to incite a riot at the convention.

Anti-war protests were happening around the world, including in Germany, known in Germany as the "'68 Movement."

* * *

During their frequent long-distance phone calls, Patrick and Clara discussed his participation in the protests and his eagerness for change.

"I'm experiencing too much anxiety," she told him, "over how the looming threat of the return of my cancer causes me to feel a persistent uncertainty for the future."

With young Patrick now in kindergarten, Clara walked all three boys to the Roberto Clemente Elementary School at the corner of Howard Avenue and Post Road (Route 1). The sleek brick, glass-and-chrome steel design offered a modern ambience and character which evoked Clara's sense of hope for her sons' futures, despite the civil unrest and the uncertainty of her health.

* * *

In April 1969, Jerome Grossman, an influential and well-known political activist, made speeches calling for a general strike across the country if the U.S. did not end its involvement in Vietnam by October. Other activists, such as Sam Brown, shifted the idea to be a broad-based moratorium, a national protest which touched every community, to create support across mainstream America beyond the hippie counterculture and the more radical leftist activists. They intended to show President Nixon, who had defeated Humphrey in the election, that a mandate existed from the people to pull U.S. troops out of Vietnam.

On October 15, 1969, the Moratorium movement launched. In Connecticut, estimates of close to 100,000 people participated across thirty-five communities to voice their support. Ten thousand people gathered in Hartford's Bushnell Park alone.

In New Haven, a smaller but sizable gathering of Yale students and New Haven residents congregated on the New Haven Green. The Green, a large sixteen-acre park in the middle of New Haven, bordered by Church, Chapel, Elm and College streets, is lined with historic buildings dating back to colonial settlers, including the library, the federal and county court buildings, several churches and hotels.

Rumors had often floated that the British spared burning down New Haven during the Revolutionary War because the Green and city surrounding it were too beautiful to destroy. The Green once again became a place of revolution and conflict during 1970.

Bobby Seale, the co-founder of the Black Panthers, went on trial in New Haven for the murder of another Black Panther leader rumored to be an FBI informant. Protestors planned a rally on the Green on May 1, 1970, to demonstrate support for Seale.

Earlier that same week, Nixon ordered U.S. troops to invade Cambodia.

The Seale support rally opened an opportunity for anti-war protestors. Shop owners locked their doors and boarded up their windows in anticipation of violence and riots. Connecticut mobilized the National Guard. Jeeps or troop carriers occupied many parts of the city.

Thousands of people showed up for the rally, including other members of the 'Chicago 8'. The crowd represented multiple interests, including Black justice and civil rights, the war in Vietnam and gender and sexual equality. Students demanded Black studies programs as well as more involvement in campus planning and governance.

The protest lasted until Sunday, May 3, when a stand-off took place between the protestors and the New Haven police chief with his policemen in riot gear, supported by National Guardsmen. Tear gas dispersed the crowd, the billowing smoke saturating the air over the Green and the nearby Yale campus. Yale organizers had hoped to keep the rally and protest peaceful by leaving the campus open and offering dormitories as shelter, which many retreated to when the tear gas filled the air.

This quiet disbursement and peaceful resolution to the military stand-off on the New Haven Green stood in sharp contrast to the violence a few days later at Kent State University where the National Guard fired live ammunition into the crowd of student protestors, killing four.

* * *

In 1972, Luigi "Gigi" Bernardo opened GiGi's Bakery on Chapel Street in New Haven. Luigi, born in Naples, Italy, in 1940, operated the bakery with his younger brothers Vincent, Alfredo and Arsenio.

In no time, Clara became one of their most frequent customers, not only because of her sweet tooth a mile long, but also because she had her eye on Arsenio. Arsenio, a tall, attractive, suave man, observed Clara shopping at the bakery. In between biscotti or cannoli, Clara and Arsenio discovered each other.

"I'm scared," Clara murmured to Arsenio. "I don't have a great record when it comes to love. It makes me anxious to think of getting involved again. A part of me has expectations, ones that have the potential to destroy this gift."

"I'm not complicated," Arsenio said in a soothing tone, "so tell me how can I help you accept me as I am, not measure me against these expectations you talk of."

"I don't know, Arsenio. But I have done it time and again, despite myself. Besides, I'm no longer the woman I used to be. My health frustrates me. I don't feel as deserving. I'm a little suspicious that you will tire of me, between my health and my demanding nature."

"I want you to let go, Clara. Allow yourself to

belong with me and be 'home' with me," Arsenio said.

The truth was, she did want to experience life with him. She loved his virtuosity, the very core of his character, which she saw as pure and inspirational. For the first time in her life, she considered not what she would get out of the relationship. It was not about the physical connection. She did not want to control or possess Arsenio, just as he did not strive to own her either. She dug deep to move forward with the relationship.

"Okay, Arsenio," Clara said, "I suppose, no matter how hard the past, you can always begin again."

Arsenio smiled. "I cherish you, Clara. You are sensuous, yet powerful. I love your confidence and strength. I don't want to do anything to change that."

Arsenio's gaze drank in Clara, sitting across the table from him. Her dazzling eyes and smile, the curvature of her cheekbones, her shapely figure, alluring but not overtly sexual. He studied her eyes, seeing past the fragility she shared with him now, looking deeper, sensing there lurked a woman waiting, full of love, power, support and intrigue. He lost his breath by her inherent beauty captured best in the dim light of the morning, the shadows and contrast accentuating her curves, electrifying the air, creating an intense, palpable intimacy in the moment. Yet, despite her repose in the morning bed, she commanded attention, aware of her very being, aware of her surroundings and of her growing comfort being vulnerable with him.

Their romance took off like a rocket. They married in 1973. Clara held Arsenio close to her heart in a way she never knew how before. They continued to do so for all thirty-seven years they shared.

Many years later, Clara reflected that her bold decision to allow Arsenio into her life and lower her defenses rewarded her every day. At the time she met Arsenio, she still carried a significant despair for an imagined past, a mourning for lost opportunities.

"I've come to recognize that the paths of life that brought Arsenio and me together in this present moment were valuable," she told a friend, "even though they were not according to plan or conforming to my ideal fantasy. I've realized the necessity of it all, that none of my experiences was frivolous or wasteful."

"Your future is not disconnected from your past, like all of us, but rather the next thing will be exactly as fated, given what you've already experienced."

This included all the multiple missteps, unpleasant moments, poor decisions, or unfortunate circumstances that were best forgotten, to be expunged from memory.

"With Arsenio, I found an internal strength to live in a more true and authentic way to who I wanted to be. I became comfortable, conscious of my vulnerability. I felt a lighthearted freedom because our space allowed me to let go. I recognized the vastness of the infinite possibilities that came from this emotional freedom."

Her friend nodded.

"There is something I want to talk with you about," Arsenio said as he approached Clara one summer day in 1979. "I think it's time to re-evaluate your relationship with Maria-Luisa."

Clara's face reddened as she resisted a vigorous shaking of her head. "You know I still have a lot of negative feelings there. What are you asking of me?"

"I've been considering everything she lived through, how different the world was at the turn of the century, also before World War I. Your mother likely did the best she could, especially trying to cope with all the changes that took place in the 1930s and 1940s."

"Are you suggesting I have to forgive her?" Clara said, squirming, yet also seeming to give a defiant answer.

"You want her to be one thing, but she is never going to be the mother that says 'good girl', so stop waiting for her to do that. You don't need her validation." Arsenio paused.

"You're right I don't." Clara nodded. "But I never felt her love or support either. Never mind the validation; I had to find love on my own terms." Forgiveness seemed one step too far for Clara.

"And how do you feel now?" Arsenio said.

"I feel complete, Arsenio, and have you to thank for that. I count my blessings every day." Clara paused, then continued, "I appreciate your pushing me, challenging me to grow more."

She at last felt fulfilled, living her own life without trying to meet the expectations and values of her mother or anyone else. Arsenio did not put labels or boundaries or controls on their love. He found comfort in their friendship and trust, as well as respect and interest in growing together.

Without having met or knowing Maria-Louisa, he maintained a similar philosophy of being in love with love itself. His friends who tried to make their "plus-one" happy ended up sacrificing so much of themselves that they were miserable in the bargain.

Arsenio had not received any formal training or traveled some exotic spiritual path, but rather possessed an innate, perhaps instinctive, understanding that his peace of mind and joy only came about by focusing on what made him feel fulfilled in all dimensions of life, the physical, spiritual, intellectual and emotional. He encouraged Clara to pursue her interests, her independence, while also keeping connected to her. He preserved a well-developed sense of self-differentiation and encouraged similar growth in Clara. As a result, they sustained an independence about what they wanted, felt, or desired, but they stayed connected, maintaining their involvement with each other at the same time.

"Home means everything to me," he told Clara, "because it's my idea of sanctuary for myself and those I love. I want it to create a sense of community, where we are happy and we develop friendships."

"I'll try, Arsenio," Clara said, "but you're aware

that all I have experienced is possession, obligation, resentment. You have tremendous capacity for compassion and forgiveness, but in my own experience, anger and conflict are dealt with through cruelty and violence, not respect or empathy."

"Kindness, to care for someone, to have compassion... all these open a door to your soul. Spend more time enjoying the church group, coaching your soccer club and managing the wedding bands," he said, "and you'll see your sense of purpose. Caring for others will create joy within you that will make love believable and trust worthy."

He admired Clara's strengths, but also exhibited purposeful tolerance of her weaknesses. He willingly put her needs before his, as she did for him. Their love became unconditional.

Arsenio tried to be a father to the three boys as well. Bobby, now twelve, had grown to be independent and considered himself the man of the house. He had been responsible for making sure Thymy and Pat got up for school, ready for the day. Bobby helped Clara clean the house and do the laundry.

Thymy, now age ten, did not respond to Arsenio. He retained a strong affiliation with his father, so now he resented Clara for breaking up the family. His anger and acting out became fuel for his drum playing and his physical fitness training as he became a teenager.

Pat, now seven years old, bonded with Arsenio almost from the start. Arsenio adopted Pat about six years later, after both Bobby and Thymy moved out. Pat credited Arsenio for instilling in him a strong sense of family, duty and responsibility.

Arsenio gave many lessons to Pat over the next several years, challenging him to understand others' points of view and to make an effort to be a better version of himself each day. Arsenio advocated for continuous learning and experiencing. He taught Pat about what a friendship means and how to look beyond the reactions or emotions in a given moment to discern a deeper connection.

"Pat, I want you to be aware how what you know and understand, along with your emotions, will have an impact on your judgment."

He coached Pat on how to think for himself, guided by his experiences and knowledge but also with a sense of higher morality. Family plus devotion were cornerstones to Arsenio's way of life, the bedrock for his sense of fulfillment and gratitude. These lessons also became guiding principles for Pat in his adult life.

"Pat, I never would have imagined my life today when I was a young man back in Italy. It is a constant thing, life, like a river that always flows, it never stops, the journey is constant."

Pat grinned at him.

"I was lucky, you see," Arsenio continued, "because I kept an open mind and open ears, I listened to what others were saying. You never know what you will learn or how you could grow as a result."

He paused, gazing at the rising steam from his espresso, taking a moment to admire the crispy texture of the shell that formed his cannoli. Being in the bakery business, aesthetic beauty was something as simple as crispy cookies or a deft swirl of piped filling.

"Life," he mused further, "is not about being perfect. That will only cause you frustration and create unnecessary challenges. Like a river, life wends and winds, it overflows its banks, it cuts curves in the land to make a new way, it flows over obstacles. It is not perfect, yet we look at it to see its beauty, its nature, because it is natural. Our history, our ancestors even, are all drops of water that start our own personal rivers. Each drop gets us here to where we are today."

He stopped to reflect further, it seemed, but in truth, it was more that he could no longer resist a taste of that cannoli. A sip of coffee afterward inspired him to say, "You see, the future will mostly take care of itself, so it will be good if you remember to be grateful and charitable and thankful regardless of your circumstances. If I had stayed in Italy, look how much I would have missed out on. I tell you, Pat, it is so important to take risks without fearing what it could be. Think 'what is the worst that could happen?' and accept that."

Arsenio tried to be practical when passing along his wisdoms, life rules and reminders. More often than not, his musings earned more eyerolls than

interest. Pat remembered some of the more important lessons, like not knocking yourself down by
being self-critical or not beingdismissive or overly
judgmental or critical of others. Be trusting instead
of controlling. Be generous and thankful for each day.
Have the grace to accept imperfection, avoid disdain,
shun being resentful.

A few years after they were married, Arsenio and
Clara moved to a split-level, two-family home with
three bedrooms on Howard Avenue. Just down the
street were the Clemente schools. The house sat
across the street from Berney's Pharmacy. The basement and backyard felt like a luxury for the children,
while Clara swooned over the washing machine. The
stairs to the second floor were straight ahead on
the left side as you walked into the house, the front
entrance opening to the living room and kitchen to
the right.

A plastic carpet guard with sharp little teeth
shielded the carpet. Plastic slipcovers protected the
couch. A floral print tablecloth covered the large
kitchen table.

Clara taught her children to clean their own
rooms. She had them wash their clothes and dry
them on the clothesline out back, using wooden pins
to hold the clothes on the line. Clara maintained a
very strict regimen for a spotless and tidy house,
flying into fits of rage if her rules were not followed.
Typical for her temper, Clara tossed all the clothes
and linens into a big pile, emptied out the offending

child's chest or closet drawers, threatening to throw away anything not put in its proper place by dinner time.

While Thymy and Pat shared a bedroom, Bobby had his own bedroom for the first time in his life, giving him plenty of space to buy and keep a vast comic book collection. He favored Marvel comic books, especially Iron Man, Thor, Shang-Chi Master of Kung Fu and Dr. Strange. He put posters of Bruce Lee on his wall. His passion for drawing expanded, so much so that he drew on the walls when he ran out of paper. He dreamed of publishing his own comic book entitled "The Dragon" or "The Condor."

One day Pat came home to discover all his comics in the garbage because Clara had found them spread out on the floor in disarray. He rescued them and stashed them away.

Howard Avenue became the birthplace for The CrossBones, the basement band the Moresco boys started. In school, they learned to play instruments. Bobby took up the piano and bass, Pat the violin and Thymy the drums. They played whatever came to mind, creating their own innovative compositions in between pastrami and cheese hoagies, with corn chips, from the deli.

Inspired more by his mother's cooking than the deli, Bobby pursued a career in the food services industry, including culinary school and management. The comic book archetype he created for himself, "The Financier," seems appropriate. Thymy, the comic book character "The Enforcer," became a mixed martial arts fighter and trainer. Pat, "The Thinker," was president of his high school chess team, became a butcher and later a grocery store manager, never too far from the pastrami and cheese.

Through her affiliation with the church, along with her passion for music, Clara managed two wedding bands that played in the area. She coordinated their schedules and booked their performances.

On Saturday mornings, she walked down the street to the corner of Court and Church to have her hair done at The Beauty Court. The salon glowed with a family atmosphere that Ann Polio, the owner, fostered with every greeting to every customer. The other stylists and women patrons mirrored her warm, open-hearted disposition. Everyone was a sister, an aunt, a cousin.

The store occupied an historic building built from brick in a Georgian architectural style, with two bay windows framing the entry. The smell of hairspray permeated the air, mixed with the chemical after-taste from perms or highlights. The hum of hair dryers that formed cones over their heads resonated along with the constant hum of chatter and laughter. The stylists worked their magic along the left side of the salon, the black chairs facing a mirrored wall.

"I enjoy sitting in the waiting area, this enclave in the bay window to the left of the door. The firm black chairs with their faux leather and spindle wood legs are just as welcoming as you are, Ann."

"We're very glad each time you're here." Ann smiled at her.

The stack of magazines that dated back years seemed to mirror the age of the building. The consistency gave Clara a sense of comfort. The rhythm mirrored the character of New Haven and the Italian community Clara identified with.

Yes, sitting there, looking out the bay window, watching the people walk by, waiting for her name to be called, chatting with the women about the children, or really whatever, in this extension of her home, this city had become her home. These people were her family.

Clara said, "I always treasure this time."

Clara loved soccer. She assisted the local soccer clubs as the doctor on the field, performing minor physical therapy, dressing injuries the players incurred, all skills she perfected after twenty years at Grace New Haven Hospital. Pat helped, too, as the water boy.

"Let me tell you about the time I watched and taped Paolo Rossi, an Italian soccer player spending some time in America playing local clubs," she said to nearby parents. "He went on to be a national team player for Italy, helping them win gold in the 1982 Olympics."

In October 1985, Clara's mother, Maria-Louisa, died. Prior to her death, Clara had travelled to Germany to be with Patrick and to spend time with Maria-Louisa while she lay ill. Even though she was indisposed, Maria-Louisa and Clara still managed to get into a heated debate. Patrick, now thirty-eight, played the part of referee. Patrizia, now a successful comedienne and actress, did not spend much time with either Maria-Louisa or Clara during this visit.

For the next fifteen years, Clara and Arsenio's life revolved around the bakery, friends, family and church. Clara continued to manage the wedding bands, as well as participate in dance contests with Arsenio. They loved to dance the Jitterbug, spinning around the dance floor, showing their youthful spirit.

Luigi Bernardo retired from the bakery and closed the business in 2001. Arsenio and Clara retired to Pompano Beach, Florida, in 2000. There, Clara once again became active in a local church community and right away established a new set of friends. They often returned to Connecticut to visit Arsenio's family and the family Bobby had started. After Luigi died in 2009, Clara and Arsenio did not travel to Connecticut as much.

Patrizia came to visit them once but the trip ended abruptly when Patrizia and Clara became embroiled in an argument about the material Patrizia used in her stand-up routine.

"It's embarrassing!" Clara shrieked at her.

Arsenio Bernardo, age seventy-six, passed away on February 3, 2010. Arsenio's whole life was one full of community and family. He volunteered, greeting each day with positive words and jokes for everyone he met. Whatever he gave came back to him in spades, due to his genuine manner. He lived a life of virtue, selflessness and integrity that attracted love through trust. He had a home in that community just as much as the home he created in Connecticut.

When he lay in the hospital, as it was clear to him the end approached, he beseeched Clara to savor every moment, be thankful and be filled with gratitude. He felt so fortunate to have those thirty-seven years with her, sharing their journey.

"I want you to see the holiness in everything and everyone around you."

Devastated by Arsenio's passing, Clara attempted to heed his words, devoting herself to the church she now belonged to, participating in the numerous works they performed in the community. She was quick to rebuke those who did not show love for others and cherished the time she spent with her grandchildren.

Arsenio always wanted to have his ashes spread across the waters near Naples, his birthplace. Clara kept the urn with the promise to spread his ashes. Perhaps one day her ashes would join his as well.

On the passing of Arsenio, Clara shared with her friends as she reflected on her life, "A passionate love, like what I had with Bobby, does not necessarily translate into a happy marriage."

Shaking her head, she told them, "Marriage needs more ingredients than just love and friendship is one of them. A solid friendship between two lovers says more about their compatibility than a passionate, ardent love affair. Arsenio was that for me."

Clara paused, gathering herself before adding, "I will be with him again someday. He wanted his ashes spread out at sea near Naples and I will have mine spread right there with him. I cannot bear to think of being anywhere else but beside him for eternity."

CHAPTER 8

Rivisitazione 1966

In November 2015, Clara received a phone call from a social worker at the adoption agency in New Haven. They had been in contact with someone looking for their biological mother. The information on file was out of date and the agency needed to verify certain details to validate the relationship between each party. The social worker requested Clara's permission for the person to send her a letter, through them, because they monitored initial contact to protect each party.

Clara agreed. On December 22, 2015, Clara received the first letter.

* * *

Dear Clara –

Almost fifty years to the day. It's hard to imagine I am actually talking with you now after all this time. This was not an easy decision for me to come to. Deciding to contact you came only recently; it has not been something I dwelled on growing up and my parents never lied to me about the adoption. This is not about reliving my life through a new lens. I find myself looking for something though, something missing. A void somewhere clouds my heart and mind.

I am on a journey and thank you for this opportunity to include you. I hope to hear back from you.

My life has been a good one. I was fortunate to have the support of two loving parents, who devoted themselves to raising me and improving our lot in life. I did not have brothers or sisters, but instead spent time with an extended family of cousins, along with aunts and uncles.

When I was very young, we moved from the New Haven area to Avon, which had, at the time, some of the best schools in Connecticut. We frequently traveled back to West Haven and Branford to visit with family. I used to spend time with my Italian grandmother and aunts in the kitchen and owe a lot of my cooking interests and style to their influence and teachings, even to this day.

My mom still lives in Avon. I lost my father to lung cancer several years ago.

I can share that my childhood was typical, one full of adventure, mischief and curiosity. We lived in a modest home, with a lawn, trees and a vegetable garden. Despite my complaints of pulling weeds, I still enjoy yard work and gardening today. I remember catching frogs and climbing trees, playing little league baseball and town soccer, spending time with friends. I played the trombone in grade school and was in the marching band. I worked hard in school and got good grades. I worked summer jobs to help pay for a private high school, which I graduated magna cum laude and went to college.

In college, I was president of the jazz band, swam on the swim team and graduated with a degree in Economics. I got work immediately and my career as a professional in insurance and health care has been fairly successful, covering almost 30 years so far.

I live in New York City now, with my wife of 21 years and our sixteen-year-old son. He is a strong, intelligent, and healthy young man. He also swims and is very excited about college, and swimming there as well. He provides a constant ray of sunshine to me and makes me laugh daily. He's turning into a very good man. I have enjoyed watching him grow, teaching him, mentoring, and coaching him.

I am proud to be his father, to celebrate his successes, and to support him in his trials. Being a good father has been very important to me.

At some point a few years ago, as I sat at home, I looked around and felt empty. Maybe it was related to the growth and maturation of my son, and feeling the emptiness his growing up will leave behind in one sense, and not fully appreciating the growth and expansion that occurs as he establishes his own life. Maybe it was triggered by the growing emotional distance and reduced frequency of seeing the rest of the family – we all have our own families and live just far enough apart that it's an effort we seldom make. Maybe it had something to do with all the time and energy focusing on my family, my career, and others, such that maybe to be happy, I needed to get back to things I have stopped, like church, music, poetry, volunteering, bike rides, swimming, soccer.

Maybe part of this emptiness actually started further back, at the beginning. I have at times, even as a child, felt adrift and disconnected from my family, using the adoption to intellectually opt in and opt out of connecting. As I have thought about these issues and their impact on my life, and the impact it's having on those I love and have loved over time, I realize it's much bigger than a mid-life crisis or a rebellion against complacency. It has been bigger than that, but hidden from me. Uncertain of the source of this ennui, I began my search, a journey to rediscover who I was and who I wanted to be.

And so, now my journey brings me to your door-step. It has already been fulfilling. The back-story of the facts and circumstances of my birth were not described or verbalized to my parents, and finding out the truth has been touching and emotional for me. I understand that time was a difficult time, but from what I learned based on limited history the adoption agency passed to me, you were strong in your convictions, had courage to make difficult deci-sions, and were foremost focused on the welfare and safety of your children.

Your strength and courage are a source of pride for me. Finding out I have (half) brothers and sisters was also very exciting and intriguing. I am anxious to know more.

How are you? I hope you are well. I understand you recently lost your husband of thirty-seven years. I am sorry for your loss. That is a remarkable stretch of time together and I imagine one filled with love, struggles, and laughter. I look forward to hearing more about your incredible journey through life, to learning more about my brothers and sisters, and to share more of myself with you.

I also understand you may be open to meeting me, to talking with me, which I realize is very sensitive, and stirs some anxiety for me as well. Many positives could come from our connecting, not just the sharing of our stories, but also the learning of your wisdom and courage throughout. I hope you will write back.

Have a wonderful and joyous Christmas,
Mark

* * *

Clara reread the letter many times. She cried tears of joy and relief. She did not know how to respond, because she felt both paralyzed and overcome with joy. The weight had been removed from her chest, a burden that had clouded her consciousness and heart for fifty years.

Clara hesitated to write back. Writing pained her because of the arthritis in her hands. Clara's health was not ideal; her legs were swollen and her breathing labored. She spent a lot of time with doctors trying to diagnose the cause of her pain and swelling. She told the agency about her health issues and the tears of joy triggered by the letter. She asked them to pass along her feelings and her request for patience in her response. After four months passed, Clara received a second letter.

* * *

Dear Clara –

I realize this is hard but I do want you to know I appreciate your effort to write me back. I hope you are feeling better. In the meantime, I thought I would write to you again.

As an only child, I have fond memories of learning to play chess with my father, and having him teach me card games. We spent hours poring through math quiz books and working pages of problems. He used the time to make sure I learned my school lessons. We did chores about the house and in the yard, and again while he was also teaching me to clean, garden, prune and weed.

I also remember playing, alone, spending time in the play area we had set up in a half-finished basement, with my Lionel trains, and GI Joe action figure, my Matchbox cars, my Legos. Oh, that bean bag frog with the Swingline logo stitched onto its chest. Playing in the yard with my Tonka trucks and building my erector sets. I still have many of these things, mementos of my childhood, and connections to my past, of happy times. I guess I am somewhat nostalgic, but then these were my "friends," who kept me company. So, of course, I held on to them, as much as I befriended the toads and frogs in the yard – capturing them and putting them in a bucket to remain safe while I cut the lawn. I suppose I was lonely, and am now realizing that I filled part of that loneliness with my vivid imagination.

Not knowing where I came from allowed me great freedom to slip between reality and imagination, as I saw fit throughout my life. I suppose to some extent I am still doing it. Sometimes this faculty is destructive and distracting, other times it can be soothing. It depends on the circumstances of the day and my intentions. Some people consider fantasy and imagination as dangerous, building mistrust in the present and making us unhappy with where we are, versus where we are not. For a substantial part of my adult life, I have turned my back on the imagination and was in fact more pragmatic, rational, focused, goal-oriented, and achievement-based. Perhaps I was just deceiving myself, as the imagination and false realities still manifested themselves in my subconscious and I was not observant; I was still fantasizing in an unconscious way.

Making a turn now, at this age, I find myself looking to reconnect with life, and with reality in whatever form it takes. I am trying to be present and authentic in my emotions. In many ways, contacting you has provided me some connection to reality. It has become for me something of a bridge back to solid ground, and not fantasy. When I have the energy and peace of mind to focus on it, I reconsider and reevaluate my life and my emotions.

My feelings for my father are a good example. Trying to teach my own son the very things my father spent so much time showing me has given me newfound appreciation for his patience, considering the complaints he must have endured. Despite his flaws, which I came to recognize as I got older and could understand what being an alcoholic meant, I loved him and he loved me. I do miss him. He passed on well before his time and I suffer from his not being part of his grandson's life. I believe I am connected to him and his passing in newfound ways that are deeper, sadder, more intense, because of the simple dialog you and I are having.

The timing for this letter is also interesting. For some time, I have been contemplating writing to you, again perhaps eager to share, perhaps excited at the possibilities, but had procrastinated. This weekend I may have received a sub-conscious "push" when my wife and I walked around the "Little Italy" section of the Bronx, during which we bought fresh pasta (cut wide – pappardelle), mozzarella, biscotti, a whole rabbit (for my ragu di oniglio for the pappardelle). Listening to older gentlemen debate the freshness of the tomatoes in the market – the young women gossiping over their cappuccinos – it felt very European and it reminded me of Grandmother and her conversations with her sisters and brothers. Cooking everything on Sunday and having the family meal over a bottle of Barbaresco completed the experience. I imagine this as not only what I encountered directly with my grandmother but also suggests what life may have been like for you as a young girl before coming to the U.S. It certainly felt comfortable and resonated of "home" to me, and very real.

Thank you, Clara, for allowing me this opportunity to share with you today. In a very unexpected way, you have already given me so much. I do hope to hear back from you soon. I am eager to know more about your life, and about you. This is all very fascinating, and I hope you are intrigued as much as you may be nervous or apprehensive after all these years.

Please be well, Clara –
Mark

* * *

Knowing that a letter would be too difficult to write and not owning a computer for e-mail, Clara instructed the agency to have Mark call her instead. Nervous and apprehensive, she did not know what to expect or what to feel.

"This has been a grace from God," she told her parish friends. "I feel light shining inside my soul. I am lifted off the ground."

At first, the conversation plodded along in an awkward dance, two strangers searching for footing, trying to find their sea legs on a rocking boat. They discussed Clara's history, her family, the time a gun was held to her head while her father played the violin. She talked about being home schooled and multi-lingual (speaking French, Italian, German and Spanish).

She described herself as a survivor, with a temper, a go-getter and a bitch. She preferred her steak on the rare side and her drinks stiff. She liked to laugh with her friends and go out to dinner. She discussed her troubled relationships, her children and Arsenio.

They touched on the painful decision to give her baby up for adoption. She still felt the tremendous burden, fifty years later.

Recounting that period of her life, Clara told Mark, "I felt trapped and betrayed by my circumstances. Here I was, a single parent with three boys already, my joys in life. Stung and bitter at 'he who shall not be named,' I had no idea I was pregnant. And then to be betrayed once again, this time by the diagnosis of ovarian cancer. The stress and financial burden were too much. And yet, I fought with the priests and the doctors alike. I did not want to accept their advice."

In the ongoing conversations, Clara discussed her other medical ailments, the surgeries on her throat and hands, the way she not long ago broke her ankle, how she survived colon cancer (doctors removed a malignancy from her small bowel) and the ovarian cancer ordeal. She discussed how her legs get swollen, when her arthritis acts up and how her right hand shakes.

They explored why he reached out to her now, after all these years. The effort to redefine himself and where his path led him. They talked about his education and professional career and his misgivings about his life at that time. They shared their respective fears and anxieties coming into the conversation, the timing and the waiting on both ends, the anticipation.

"After the adoption," he told Clara, "my mother got pregnant again, despite doctor's warnings against it. She had had three prior miscarriages and another was feared to be life threatening. This fourth pregnancy also ended with a miscarriage and very severe hemorrhaging. The nurses' notes revealed she survived solely because she possessed the will to go home to care for the child she had just adopted."

Clara loved this story. It was comforting to her to hear about things that were miracles to her. It affirmed her faith in God.

They discussed the essay contest that his son won

and also shared photos. Their frequent phone conversations morphed into almost-daily text messaging. In those messages, Clara often referred to Mark as her son.

"Clara, you know I have a mother, a loving woman and family who raised me. There's a higher requirement than giving birth to define someone as a mother. I don't feel it's right or appropriate for you to do that."

"Why do you try to hurt me," she wailed. "What did I do to deserve this malicious attack?"

It was clear at that moment that Clara could not understand the discovery phase he was going through, as he got in touch with feelings of abandonment he still needed to process and reconcile.

"You coming back to me is my salvation, a blessing," she told him. "I love you."

"I hear you say that, Clara and I feel like you want to take a victory lap," Mark said. "The true glory, however, is your strength and courage to have made a difficult but correct decision fifty years ago."

Although he gave Clara credit for her choice, he was still processing a lifelong struggle with lack of self-esteem and a newly-found appreciation for the way abandonment and fear of attachment had shaped his life. Atonement was not needed, just understanding and reflection.

This healing process continued.

One day, Clara opened up about her mother. "She was my mother and I loved her and I hated her, too.

She was abusive and, in the end, a cold and unapproachable, unavailable mother."

Clara paused, her voice wavering. "Her love was best expressed through pain and anger. Often it took on a physical form. A beating was the only way I figure she remembered that I was her daughter."

Clara spared no details of the way this relationship established the baseline for her understanding about what love looked like. It shaped how Clara set expectations for what she deserved and what she was willing to accept from others.

Clara's failing health became a centerpiece of their conversations. "Mark, I'm sorry I cannot talk more today, I have yet another migraine and my arthritis in my ankles hurts me so much. I just want to lie down."

"Has the shaking in your hand eased?" Mark said, fearing that Clara was also at the onset of Parkinson's.

"It comes and goes," she said in a somber tone. "I don't think I will be able to drive much longer."

"How will you be able to get around and go to church or the hairdresser? Is there a town shuttle?"

"Pat and his family lived here with me for a while, but his family is growing and he needs more space for them. Then Thymy moved in when Pat moved out and he and his wife are helping me now."

"How is that working out?" said Mark.

Clara had talked about her relationship with her sons before and how strained it became at times. It was a palpable mix of love and hate, of emotional manipulation and control, of conflict between a strong-willed and dominating mother in relation to the equally-determined women her sons had married. While Clara expressed motherly concerns, it seemed she remained childish in her desire to be the center of attention, especially given her health. In many regards, she still embodied that precocious teenager, dancing in the middle of the dinner party in Stuttgart once again. Arsenio's passing left a hole that Clara had not been able to fill on her own.

Clara told Mark, "I have given up on being happy. I just want to be at peace."

"I'm sorry you are having these challenges, Clara," Mark said, "but at least you see your friends or go to church. That gives you some comfort and spiritual and emotional fulfillment to offset your physical pain."

"Yes, Mark, it does," she said, "but when I get sick or don't feel well, then I am unable to attend church events or see friends," Clara sighed. "And then all these physical challenges become more oppressive, more real, my passing to the Lord's care more apparent."

In moments like this, Clara became quiet, losing the spirit to do much of anything except stay in her room and watch television. Some days she felt anxiety because she wanted to do more but she also saw her time slip away. She loved Arsenio, but on certain days she resented his death and the feelings of abandonment it triggered. She had many fantasies of what old age would be like with three sons and an adoring husband to dote over her. She struggled with her disillusionment.

"I have suffered much of my life," Clara told Mark, tsk-tsking, "and struggled with challenges... so many challenges. I suppose suffering is a part of life, so ignoring it or denying it would only be frustrating. I am fortunate each struggle was a challenge not to just tolerate or endure it, but survive it and grow from it. The hardest part was to avoid the lingering sense of failure or despair that Fate was somehow stacked against me."

"You were not always patient, though, were you?" Mark said.

"No, at times I was very frustrated. But I always tried to be diligent and persistent and faithful when facing adversity. I read the Bible, I looked to James and Nehemiah and the teachings about perseverance being the gift that pain or despair gives us, leading us to the light (of faith)."

"Why is your religion so incredibly important to you, Clara?"

"In my church and in my parish, it is the people who are my religion," she said. "I found support that reinforces my faith in God through the humanity and compassion we share within that community."

"I have a question for you, Mark." She inhaled, then let out her breath in a deep sigh. "Why do you think you have such a hard time finding happiness?

Why do you hurt so much?"

"You know, Clara, I don't have a good answer for you," Mark said, wincing. "I've struggled with low self-esteem my whole life, with self-inflicted wounds to show for it. Anxieties and frustrations swirl around unwavering ambitions and ideals for what life should be about. A certain restlessness and disturbance roil the water and agitate me. I am sad knowing how much it has hurt those around me and in my life."

"I see you as a gentle and patient man," Clara said, nodding, "You tolerate much internally and yet you find the space to be generous and compassionate, caring more for others than for yourself. Do you not see how much you are loved for the person you are?"

"Thank you for your kind words, Clara, but I have a hard time accepting these virtues. I know I have a long and difficult journey ahead. I need to change my perspective of myself and overcome what I can only describe as a sense of self-contempt."

He hesitated there, not wanting to conclude the thought. As he faced Clara, he knew she would never acknowledge her role, along with the circumstances beyond their control, that had created this internal storm.

Instead, he continued. "One thing I have learned, Clara, through you, is that I should be recognizing challenges as opportunities for growth and something to be grateful for."

Clara saw herself in Mark as well. She held onto many things in her past. But interacting with Mark, even if only through text messages, gave her some relief. She no longer felt like a prisoner of her past. She shed the feelings of self-incrimination, especially related to the adoption. She felt more peaceful than she had in years.

"I have struggled against what seemed like endless challenges," she kept telling Mark, "and I always prayed for the wisdom and strength to see things through. But you, my son, you were sent by God to help me. You have given me peace once again."

Mark bristled at her self-proclaimed salvation and the conflict he felt at helping her reconcile her guilt and give her an internal forgiveness.

"God's mercy and his agents are everywhere," she said, "so don't be fooled by what they look like or be foolish to reject them because you will only suffer more."

In June of 2017, Mark traveled to Florida to visit Clara. Before meeting her, he spent a few days collecting his thoughts and calming his anxieties, playing out all the possible different scenarios for how this first physical meeting could go. It was important to him to establish boundaries, but to also find enough latitude to accept Clara for who she is and to understand when she may not give him the space he wanted.

He needed to make her understand how he felt uncomfortable when she called him "son," a right he reserved for his mother, who had raised him and fed him and taught him about life. Wringing his hands and rubbing his temple, he replayed the scene over and over, familiarizing himself with the difficult balance of facing that potential conflict and yet still being able to assert himself with compassion.

Clara also had some misgivings. "Thymy, I am excited and nervous," she told her son. "What does he think he will get from me and will I be able to give it to him? All I know is I feel a part of me is coming back to me and it brings me so much joy," she sobbed.

Thymy patted her shoulder, holding her in his arms. "It'll be okay, Mom. You'll see. This is important for you. I was too young back then to know what happened, but I'm glad to know this part of your life now."

Thymy faced life with a brave face, a toughened exterior, a strength and bravado that Clara found calming.

The doorbell rang. Thymy opened the door.

"Hi, I'm Mark," said the man standing at the door. "Is Clara home?"

"Come on in. I'm Thymy and this is Clara," he said sweeping his hand toward the living room beyond the open door.

Clara stepped forward, beaming, her blue eyes twinkling in the afternoon light, as she reached her hands out for Mark's, a tear rolling down her cheek.

Clara lived in a quiet two-bedroom condominium, with oak-paneled kitchen cabinets, white tiled floors and a small garden out back. Her living room furnishings included a couch and a couple of side chairs centered around a coffee table. A credenza along the wall displayed figurines and mementos, religious artifacts and pictures. The urn with Arsenio's ashes was there as well.

Once Mark settled on the couch, Clara sat in the chair to his left and Thymy joined them, choosing the chair to Mark's right.

Despite all the misgivings and worries, their meeting turned into a normal afternoon.

"I worried for no reason," Mark mused to himself. "I think I remember something Seneca said, we suffer more in our imagination that in reality."

Indeed, their time together proved loving and calming, with results of a common understanding across shared experiences, even though they had travelled different paths. They discovered a unity and a bond that they both desired and vowed to continue to develop.

Clara referred to meeting Mark as "being in her glory," not that she claimed rights to his success or well-being, but rather the peace and tranquility knowing that when she made the difficult choice so many years ago, she did the right thing. Realizing that by itself had merit and glory to it.

The meeting was also a success in reducing the residual emotional distance between them, though

Mark remained hesitant and wary of Clara's possessiveness and tendencies toward emotional manipulation.

Clara's failing health soon tested them both.

CHAPTER 9

Di Nuovo il Cancro

Prior to Arsenio, Clara had allowed healthcare issues and financial concerns to consume her life. At that stage, she did not have the luxury or time to be soft, compassionate, or even very human. Her history and experiences did not accommodate sympathy or the vulnerability for love in any true sense.

In her survival mode, post-World War II, she knew the "how" behind "be loving"—meaning the actions, the motions, what to do or say, including how to be a parent. Adept in the acts of offering kindness and care, she performed her duty and responsibilities.

She mastered "doing" without much thinking about emotions or realizing what it meant to love, or to be connected. She walled herself off, hardened against compromise or acceptance. She pursued injurious relationships where she connected two elements, friendship and lust and equated this combination to be love.

Arsenio had changed her life, as well as her

thoughts about what life could be and the person she could become, while her faith was a constant throughout.

Clara practiced her faith every weekend. It validated her faith to witness or read stories that showed compassion, sympathy, gentleness, or love.

"It made me cry," she told Mark, "to see the looks of appreciation and surprise on the faces of the people we served today."

"Your ministry and weekends with your parish give you a lot, help you feel better about yourself."

"It helps me because it offers me something to believe in."

"Maybe," Mark said, "it's just enough to give you and your friends hope that somewhere there was something worthy of belief or faith."

"I am strong and stubborn,"—Clara gritted her teeth—"and I certainly do not need to rely on anyone else to take care of me. I believe in myself, first and foremost. But my faith also reminds me that while I am self-sufficient, others are always there walking alongside me, whether I acknowledge them or not."

She paused to take a deep breath. "I have learned this too late, but I hope my children will see the endless possibilities that are present now, today and not wait for the future so much."

"We have a role to play." Mark picked up where she hesitated once more, searching for her words. "We are all connected, we have to be there for each other, listen to each other."

"Yes, yes," she gushed, giddy, more animated than Mark ever heard her. "It is easy enough to be consumed and complain about things or to be self-involved, but we share this one life, the blessings we have are meant to be shared, no matter what they are."

Clara continued into her usual diatribe about the grace of God and the wonders of His works. It was a strong faith and a comfort to her on her most trying days.

Clara withstood many days filled with physical pain plus a constant concern about her financial condition. Perhaps it was her faith, or her reflection on her life, but in conversations with Mark she seemed to rally enough to consider herself fortunate. She gave credit to her higher power for the gift of perseverance and endurance that allowed her to survive, even thrive, despite the pain and sorrow she experienced, along with her bittersweet experience with Love.

"Mark, I hope to encourage you so I pray you will one day recognize and appreciate what is before you," she said. "I worry about you, all these anxieties and fears, the uncertainties. What do you think you need for your happiness?"

"I am looking for that answer, Clara, trying to find the right balance. Intellectually, my work is challenging and stimulating, so I'm passionate about it. It's fulfilling in many ways, even on an emotional level, to an extent. The joy or fulfillment is from really investing myself, giving myself to the effort. It is not about wealth and material possessions, or pride and reputation. Still, something is missing. Therefore, I have been getting back to taking care of myself more, eating better and exercising, so physically I'm improving, with more to do."

"But you are lacking emotional and spiritual joy." Clara almost snapped at him. "I can sense that much better than you can. It is very clear to me now."

"That is true, especially the emotional part. I go to museums and find other avenues to achieve some sense of spiritual fulfillment. Recognizing beauty and I mean the pure aesthetic—"

"I know what you mean!"

"...I am seeing it, recognizing in everything. I sense it, which lets me acknowledge it sometimes when I am not weighed down by something else, some stress or anxiety."

"My dear, I understand so I'm very happy for you. You may look at me, living in my bedroom, with only a TV and my rosary," she said, "and ask yourself, 'what kind of life is this?', but I tell you every day gives me an opportunity to see wonders and beautiful things. It is so important to find joy today. I am ready, you know. They can take it all, I will let go of all the things that can be taken, but I will hold fast to my feelings when the warm sun is on my face, when I hear the laughter of my friends, or savor the smell of homemade tomato sauce on the stove."

She paused again and Mark wondered if she was crying.

"It has not been an easy road," she continued, "because even being in love—that, I learned is fleeting, too, by the way—even love was not what I envisioned. Only after possessing it did I realize how very different it was from what I expected. Yet, like the leaf colors during autumn, it is something appreciated because summer has left, so now I enjoy the explosion of colors that signify the change of seasons. Nothing is permanent, it is always in motion, as Arsenio would say, so appreciate today and have hope for tomorrow. Change and adversity help us understand better how to cherish those moments where we allow joy."

Clara and Mark talked or sent text messages to each other daily. Clara enjoyed calling Mark ten minutes after midnight on the eve of his birthday to be the first to wish him happy birthday, a day she vowed she would never forget. They commiserated over Clara's frequent migraines, the pending thunderstorms in Florida and which son was the latest to not return her phone call within her rapid expectations. They talked about the Valentine's Day gifts she received (French and Italian chocolates and a sequined blouse, which she was both excited by and a little embarrassed). They chatted about food, what they cooked, what they ate last night, what restaurant they visited.

On weekends they discussed more of her past, the struggles she had faced. She did not like to share anything about her failed relationships. They deliberated about her children and their lives. She worried about them, at times striving to understand why they seemed angry with her. She loved to describe going to church, involving herself in the Sunday activities. She listened intently about Mark's participation in his church choir.

A typical day ended with a text from Clara. "Good night, my dear, I love you, have a pleasant night. Like I said, don't ever forget that you are always in my thoughts and in my heart. God bless you. I love you, have a sweet night and pleasant dreams."

She experienced the greatest happiness discussing a night out with her friend Linda and the movies they saw. They had treated themselves to dinner at Red Lobster afterward.

Clara loved to gossip about Maria Callas, whom she called a "number one witch," a diva who treated her and her mother, Maria-Louisa, terribly, taking on the airs of a prima donna, delving into temper tantrums the moment she did not get exactly what she wanted. Still, she confessed she loved Callas' performance of La Traviata.

Clara told Mark all about her brother, Patrick Strub, and his wife, Gisela. Clara shared a picture of Patrick, Gisela and their two daughters, Angelika and Frederica, who were also musicians. When Gisela received a diagnosis of cancer, Clara often called Patrick to support him. She also soothed Mark when his mother was taken to the intensive care unit after a car accident. Clara commiserated with the condition of his mother and her anger over her own loss of mobility. She encouraged patience and understanding because it would be a difficult transition, as she had experienced herself.

They shared family pictures of current events, a high school graduation, a dinner party, a weekend by the pool. Clara discussed her stress and anxiety about losing her independence, not being able to drive any more, having shoulder surgery to repair her rotator cuff. Her medications sometimes caused her to be sleepy so she apologized at length in her next text message for having missed sending a good night or being late with her good morning.

The following are selected texts Clara and Mark shared during 2018-2021.

June 11, 2018

M: Good morning, Clara. Mom has been through a couple of additional procedures most recent one to repair the lens on her eye. There are some complications. The knee seems to be doing OK. As for me, lots of stress. Many things going on at the same time. It's really challenging to keep it all together. Many of the items that impact the business are outside my control so that's frustrating. I think I have been ignoring the stress a bit, walling myself off from it. I'm good at that, protecting myself emotional involvement. It all has me thinking now what else I may be hiding from or have walled up and put aside.

C: Good morning, my dear Mark. I am sorry you are having stress issues. I am praying and hoping it will be easier and better for you. Don't get discouraged. I know there are certain moments when one feels that no matter what you do, it feels impossible to cope with. Please do not give up and get down. You do not give up; you are a person with stamina and willingness to do what you aim for and I admire that in you. I know it is easier said than done, but you are strong and you have the willpower to follow through. Do what you think has to be done and don't let anybody tell or influence you. I'm glad your mom is doing well. I am sending you my love with strength and blessings.

August 1, 2018

C: I am watching America's Got Talent – do you watch it? I love this show. And tomorrow is World of Dance, I enjoy watching the dancing like Dancing with the Stars. I guess it's time to say good night, I hope you sleep with sweet dreams and a blessed night. Sending you all my love and prayers with all the blessings, my dearest Mark.

M: Hi Clara – Yes, we watch AGT and the dancing shows, too. Mom's eyesight is coming back slowly and she is happy about that, but her knee is starting to bother her. Let me know how Thymy, Bobby and Pat are. Good night, Clara.

Thursday, January 31, 2019

C: My doctor told me they found 2 masses in my left breast and need to go for a biopsy to find out Monday. Please don't say anything to Thymy or Pat. I don't want anyone else to know until I find out more. This brings memory and fear back to me but thank God I have strong belief in Him and I know he will help me again and nobody can stop me from believing that

M: Clara – I am sorry to hear about those masses. Are you very concerned? Are these related to your prior cancer and the remission?

Monday, February 4, 2019

C: Before I say good night, I tell you that I am having 3 biopsies on the 18th so you know I am upset and yes I know I am not supposed to worry but I am and I can't stop. God bless you and be protected by your angels.

M: Clara, I know these things create a lot of anxiety for you – please keep me up to date. I will pray for you and the favorable outcome, maybe benign or fibroid diagnosis. Goodnight Clara.

Wednesday, February 20, 2019

C: We did 2 of the 3 biopsies today. It was bigger than they expected. The Dr thinks it is definitely cancer infected, no doubt. I am not happy and want to scream 'not again'.

M: Oh no, Clara, did they mention what stage they thought it may be? I will pray for you Clara – I hope the improved technology like cyber-knife will help you get heal faster and better than you experienced in the past.

Thursday, March 21, 2019
C: Hi Mark. I am having my surgeries on 9 of April and then after 4 weeks I will begin radiation therapy and then I will have to take some pills for how long I do not know – how are you? Are you ok? Have you cooked anything special lately?

M: Hi Clara. I have been sick with stomach virus the past few days – cooking is chicken broth lol nothing special about that. How are you – are you anxious about the surgeries?

C: Yes oh yes I am. I wish I could sleep without dreaming about the past when I was struggling with my health and with what I have to do. I can't believe that I lived in such turmoil. I can't believe I went through such pain. I just thank God that he pulled me through and helped me to survive and helped my child to get a wonderful life and was loved. I am thankful and grateful that he heard my cries and prayers. So now everything is coming back to me and

I am full of fear that will not be a very good time for me.

Tuesday, April 9, 2019
C: Good night, Mark. I had my surgery and I am in a lot of pain and I am home. My doctor gave me some morphine for pain and it helps a bit. I am going to sleep now. God bless you, sending you my prayers.

M: Wow, the good news Clara is you are home and the surgery went well. Please be careful with that morphine. I'm glad you recently had a visit with Pat and Thymy and the grandchildren. God speed in your recovery Clara – and hopefully the margins are clean or benign. Good night, Clara.

Saturday, April 20, 2019
C: I have good news, Mark. The tests came back and it looks like they got most of it. I do not need additional surgeries. Now I can start my radiation and medicine. I am aware the cancer could act up again but I am hopeful the radiation will do the trick.

M: That's great news Clara! Happy Easter!

Monday, May 20, 2019
C: Well, Mark, prayers and well wishes are not working too good. The doctors say the cancer has spread and I will most likely have chemo. The lymphedema treatment is very painful. I am very

upset. Right now I am just going to lay down and rest. My dear Mark, I hope you understand that, you are in my heart and mind.

M: I can only imagine how hard this is, Clara. This all must remind you of the process you went through before, after I was born, being exhausted and all that.

C: My lawyer and priest and my doctor helped me the most at that time. Now I have my Church, my pastor and his wife and my friends praying for me. Tomorrow I have an MRI and another treatment. I will say good night now. Good night and pleasant dreams, my dear Mark.

Tuesday, May 21, 2019
Good morning, Clara. I have a semi busy day... there's always just a few more things... I hope you continue to have strength and faith, Clara. I know this time is hard and painful and tiring. Please keep a good diet. I am saddened to see you go through all this because I know the toll cancer treatment took on my father. You are in my thoughts and prayers for a full recovery and peace. When is the next time they evaluate you to see if the treatment is working? I hope you are getting some rest to offset the pain and discomfort you have been experiencing.

Friday July 26, 2019

C: My dear Mark, I have a meeting with my two doctors and they will be doing radiation with the chemo for 3 weeks or so. They are afraid the cancer in the lymph nodes will spread and move forward. I will know more in a few weeks. My brother is fearful about Gisela, her chemo is not working out. For them, all I can do is pray. I am just so upset for me and for Gisela.

M: Thanks for keeping me up to date on what's going on, Clara. It's unfortunate and troubling... I continue to pray for you and hope that gives you some comfort. The lymph nodes are a dangerous place for cancer, it's like through the body like a super highway. I am so sorry you are having to go through this.

Sunday August 4, 2019

M: Good morning, Clara. I hope you feel well enough to get to church today. Spending time with those friends is very important – have you been able to eat or your throat still bothering you?

C: Good morning. No, I have been ill to my stomach all night so church is out and yes, my throat is bothering me very much. I am just so sensitive I don't know I am getting very annoyed and I still have more sessions and then I might do chemo but I am thinking to stop all of it. I have had enough of all of it and I am frustrated. I'm going to lay down again.

Monday August 5, 2019
M: I hope you had a peaceful rest last night, Clara. I know this is all very hard and painful. Whether they say it or not, I know Pat, Thymy and Bob are with you in spirit and love you. You know I also care about you and the church community and your friends are always so supportive. You do not walk alone. Have the doctors said anything about the progress you are making? How will they know when the cancer is in remission or is still active or spreading? It's a concern I'm sure we all have.

Tuesday, August 6, 2019
C: Good morning, my dear. I am hopeful for some news today. I am tired of the whole thing and I am getting to the point to stop all medication and let nature take his course.

Wednesday August 7, 2019
C: I received news. It's not great. I am not in remission. The cancer is still there. They gave me pills to take instead of chemo at my age. Please my dear, don't worry I am in good hands and I am honored that you worry about me that much. The only side effect I have is being tired. I am going to sleep now. Good night, my dear Mark.

M: Good morning, Clara. I am disappointed

to hear that the radiation has not eradicated the cancer. I knew it was a long shot given the proximity of the breast cancer to the lymph nodes. What did the doctor say he expected the pills to do? Be safe with hurricane Dorian that's coming, Clara - my thoughts and prayers are with you.

Sunday September 29, 2019

C: Did you go sing today? I hope you did because I know how happy that makes you. I am freezing all the time ever since I had radiation. I spent time at Linda's house. I am just so tired of it all and could just call it quits I am tired of it all. My dear Mark, sleep well.

M: Good morning, Clara. You had a lovely visit with your friend Linda. I can only imagine how frustrating things have been for you lately. So it was good that you were able to spend some time away and enjoy the company. Will the weather be ok for you to sit outside and get some sunshine? I did sing Sunday and had a chance to take a nap. It was relaxing.

Monday November 4, 2019

C: I am in a lot of pain today, my dear Mark. That's what I have to endure. I have to go for a full body scan because the doctor thinks the cancer may have spread.

M: Hi Clara – you must be very frustrated by the

delay until the 21st in addition to the persistent pain and discomfort. You have a lot to deal with.

Monday November 11, 2019
M: Happy Birthday, Clara! Did your friends take you to dinner? Hope you got a chance to get out and get away from the pain and frustrations and enjoy some part of your day today.

C: Yes, my dear, we had a nice time. We went to Red Lobster it was very nice. I am tired now and will lay down.

Sunday November 24, 2019
C: Hi, my dear Mark. I hope you had a beautiful day and sang nice hymns. I was not unhappy to not be able to go to church. I was talking with my brother and feel so bad for him. Without Gisela, he is lost and I know how he feels. I feel the same way after I lost Arsenio and I pray to him every night and I miss him terribly. Good night, my dearest Mark, sleep well.

M: Thanks Clara, have a good night. Hope your test results from the bone scan are finally available this week and you get some good news.

Sunday December 15, 2019
M: Hi Clara. I am sending you some pictures of our church and a recording of the hymns we sang in mass because you couldn't get to church. It's pretty

all decorated for Christmas. Have a blessed day, Clara.

C: The pictures are absolutely beautiful and I want to thank you so much. I was feeling tired a bit and let myself down without reason Xmas is always a difficult time for me since my husband died. I keep missing him and not being in a good mood. And now my drs' nurse called and I have to go in for a liver test but I never had anything wrong with my liver.

M: Ok Clara. Maybe they are concerned about liver damage from the medication. Is there an outside chance they are looking for new malignancies?

Tuesday December 24, 2019
M: Merry Christmas Clara – we sing tonight at the midnight mass. I will record the singing for you. I hope you have a blessed and peaceful Christmas Clara.

C: I hope you had a wonderful Christmas mass tonight and wish you all the best you are in my thoughts and in my heart. God bless you, my dearest Mark.

Monday January 6, 2020
C: The news is not good. The tests came back positive. I am very upset and so are my doctors they were hoping my tests were clear but no they came back

positive and you know I am just so tired and drained from crying, I feel as the world is lost to me. I have to go to bed now and calm down. I pray every night for God to give me strength to face the facts and see the beauty in every person. Sleep well and pleasant dreams my dearest Mark.

M: Good morning, Clara. I am also upset and disappointed to hear this news. I am sorry you are having such a difficult time and continue to face even more treatment. Can they do anything to manage the pain?

Wednesday January 29, 2020
C: I went to see my doctor and had a very intense exam. They are going to do a biopsy on my lower back because there were some shadows in the bines that makes me very nervous. I am going to pray for my brother who needs some surgery. I am going to rest a while now.

Monday February 24, 2020
M: I will pray for you and a favorable biopsy. Thank you for keeping me up to date on Patrick's condition and glad to hear he is doing well. We are well and I hope you are able to get some rest and have less pain now with the pain management.

Wednesday March 11, 2020
M: Clara – I hope you are staying safe and taking

precautions against the spread of the COVID virus. I know Florida may not be seeing a lot of cases right now but it's a big deal in NYC. Have you heard anything on your biopsy?

C: My dearest, I was going to text you but I did not want to upset you. The news is not good. I have bone cancer and the doctors said they have to switch medication and do more radiation. I wish the good Lord would just call me to end this life so I can have a beautiful life with Him. That's my wish. I will talk more later, my dear Mark.

M: Oh no Clara – did they mention what they thought the prognosis is? Have you discussed palliative care? Rest, Clara and try to find some peace in all this. My prayers are with you.

Sunday April 12, 2020
M: Happy Easter Clara!

C: Happy Easter, my dearest Mark. I hope you have a blessed day with your family

Saturday April 25, 2020
M: Good Morning, Clara how are you doing? Nothing really going on here – we are well and weathering through the pandemic as best we can. We stay home and keep busy. I do my yoga every morning. I sing along to some YouTube videos because we cannot

go into churches to sing right now. Are you ok? Are you concerned about the re-do of the bone scan? Do they think it got worse, despite the medications?

Friday May 1, 2020
M: Clara – I hope you receive this message – I heard about your massive stroke last night. I spoke with Pat and Thymy. You are in my thoughts and prayers – May God be with you and give you a quick recovery. Everyone is concerned for you and your well-being. I hope you can feel that and use it as fuel to get better.

Mark did not hear back from Clara. He kept in touch with Pat and Thymy to understand what was going on and how Clara was doing. He recalled a prayer that Clara shared as being one of her favorite comforts.

Dear Lord, the spring of everlasting light, pour into the hearts of your faithful people the brilliance of your eternal splendor, that we may have the darkness of our souls dispelled and so be counted worthy to stand before you.

Chiara (Clara) Moresco Banardo succumbed to her illness on February 5, 2021, after a prolonged coma and two strokes. She died ten years plus a day after the love of her life, Arsenio, passed away.

Clara Moresco-Bernardo

CHAPTER 10

Tornado a Casa

The plane landed at Fiumicino Airport in Rome, on time, without any turbulence. As the wheels touched down, some passengers applauded, some put their rosaries away, while others just yawned off the effects of the overnight flight from Atlanta International.

Pat and his family gathered their reading materials and electronics. Pat was amazed at how many things were strewn about, even though each child was restricted to a single backpack. It dawned on him that this was the first trip they had taken as a family to a foreign nation, never mind that they were in Italy.

Pat watched his oldest son, Jake, help his youngest daughter, Madison, get her things together. He smiled to see the young man emerging before him, who had recently started his own life in Boston with friends from college.

"When are Thymy and Bobby supposed to be here?" Pat's wife, Tiffany, said.

It was a good question. Planning this trip had been difficult to near impossible.

"I haven't heard back from Thymy about his flight. He mentioned something about having a hard time getting off work, plus he really is not comfortable flying, plus flights from Florida were expensive. He seemed hesitant and I didn't want to wait any longer. I'm hoping Bob got out of Chicago at least. I checked the weather and the storms there seemed pretty bad."

"Are you okay doing this by yourself?" Tiffany said, as she tugged on his sleeve.

"I have my family with me, which means all the world to me," Pat said with a nod.

His reply was mostly true. Inside, it stung a bit to think his brothers would not join him.

"Besides," he continued, "I have no control over any of this. It is what it is."

Pat smirked. He knew how much his brothers bristled whenever he said that.

Pat reached into the overhead bin to remove his backpack. He unzipped it with slow caution to make sure nothing had been broken or spilled. After confirming that everything was safe and secure, he shepherded everyone off the plane. "Come on, guys, follow the people – we have to go through Italian immigration. Everyone have their passports?"

As fortune would have it, they all did, nothing was lost mid-flight, no phones left behind.

Success, he thought.

Many of the people in front of them seemed to know right where to go. The signs were multi-lingual, but being on foreign soil disoriented him. The lines through immigration moved at a quick pace. They proceeded to the luggage carousel to retrieve their checked suitcases.

"There's mine!" squealed Madison, still innocent, bubbling with the joyous possibilities of life and the excitement of this adventure.

Pat all but sprinted to retrieve it. He also spotted their other three bags among the crowded carousel.

"Okay, now we need to find the train. We are looking for the Leonardo Express. That takes us to Rome where we need to transfer to a different train, so don't get too comfortable. When we reach the Rome station, we'll have some time to grab lunch before our next train at 5:30."

"Are we going to have dinner in Rome then?" whined Pat's teenaged son, Brad. "That's kind of late."

Pat rolled his eyes. *Here we are in Italy and their first thought is about food.*

"Everything is a little different here. We will be in Naples by 8:30, which will be perfect to check in to the hotel, then get dinner. I'm sure there will be something interesting and delicious to eat in the Rome train station. It's Rome, after all!"

Pat waited for the weight of the situation, along with the words, to resonate. A shrug of their shoulders had to suffice.

The shuttle from the airport into the city went without any fuss and true to Pat's predictions, the most difficult thing was choosing a restaurant. Everything smelled so good and everyone had a big appetite. The excitement of the trip now more prevalent in their mood and energy levels as the compression of the plane wore off.

After lunch, they found the correct track and boarded around 5:00. Pat placed their luggage in the storage area. They took seats along one row, with someone looking out of a window on either side of the train.

The train pulled away from the station on time, gliding down the tracks through Rome toward Naples. The tiled roofs and plastered walls looked different than their neighborhood back in Georgia. The buildings gave way to verdant green pastures and distant hills.

The children pressed against the glass to stare at the tremendous stone aqueduct on the way toward Torricola.

"That thing is huge!" gushed his teenaged daughter, Julia.

At least they are not asking about food now.

Each town along the route repeated the pattern. Expansive farms and rolling green hills, then stone ruins, followed by a town or small city, then more rolling green hills. As the train approached Latina, the Castello Caetani de Sermonetta, carved into the mountain to the east, came into view.

"Why are there so many castles around here?" said Madison.

"Many, many years ago, this area was not one country," said Pat. "I learned about this myself only recently. There were a lot of different kingdoms and rulers, plus many wars. Italy was a very divided place. The result was, everyone built a castle to protect the land and people they ruled over."

"Why isn't it like that anymore?"

"Well, I suppose people got tired of all the conflicts and just wanted to be part of one country, especially since they all share the same language and culture."

Pat gazed out the window at the rolling hills on one side, the Mediterranean Sea just beyond, the rising mountains to the other side. Something welled up inside him, a feeling he did not anticipate. He could not resist observing how untouched this land was, for hundreds of years, or even longer.

This is what makes people fall in love with Italy, he thought as he sighed.

As the train rounded the bend at Cicerone in its approach to Vindicio and Formia, the wide Mediterranean stretched before them. The setting sun illuminated Castello Angioino-Aragonese like a diamond floating over the brilliant blue waters.

"Half-way there," murmured Pat as he pointed out the window.

No one heard him mention the itinerary in his absent-minded tone. They stood transfixed.

As the train approached Naples, in the distance

Mt. Vesuvius emerged.

"Are we going to tour Pompeii and see the ruins from the eruption?"

"Yes, while we are here, I think that would be something we should do," Pat said.

As the train pulled into Napoli Centrale, they were once again uprooted from fascination and wonderment. Pat coaxed each one of them to grab their bags and note their belongings, because it would be a disaster to have anything lost at this juncture.

They left the station, roller bags rumbling behind them, plodding through the Piazza Giuseppe Garibaldi. A huge statue of Garibaldi in the center of the plaza loomed before them.

"This Garibaldi guy must have been important," Pat's son said.

"Yeah, I guess so," said Pat with a shrug.

The bustle of the shoppers, cars, buses and street performers, along with the tantalizing aromas from the restaurants lining the Piazza, were dizzying and amazing.

They checked into their rooms at the Palazzo Caracciolo Napoli. Once the youngest took her turn jumping onto the bed and the mystery of the bidet was solved (and the giggles subsided), Pat and his family strolled a short distance to the nearby restaurant that the doorman had recommended.

"The hotel is very nice, but you should see Naples first," he told them. "Just down the street, around the corner, sit outside, enjoy Italy," he said as he pointed, "and you can't miss it, just opposite Castel Capuano! Bona sera!"

Figlia d'O Luciano was just as the doorman had described. Pat felt rejuvenated after finishing his linguini ai frutti di mare and everyone else seemed satisfied.

"Tomorrow," he said, "we will be taking a cab down to Castle Ovo, where we can wander around and see one of these castles up close. But remember, we are going there to be near the sea. It is important to me to honor Nonna's last wish."

"Do you think Thymy or Bob will make it in time?"

"I don't know. So maybe one of you can film me as I sprinkle Arsenio's together with Nonna's ashes. That way, we can share it with them even if they can't be here with us."

Pat felt a sudden, small stab of fatigue. He played out the day tomorrow in his head. The urns with Clara's and Arsenio's ashes were still in his backpack. They always wanted to be put into the sea off the coast of Naples together.

She will finally have her peace, he thought, trying to console himself. *Clara will have returned to her heart's home.*

Something deep inside told him they all had.

EPILOGUE

Once upon a time there was a girl who met a boy. The spark between them became a flame that, through magic and love, turned into another little girl. The family lived and laughed, danced and flickered brilliance against looming shadows.

Darkness almost engulfed the three of them many times. But the little flame that became a girl would not be deterred. She re-ignited time and again, sharing her power with her children while spreading her light wherever she could. She cast her own shadow, of course, because a shadow always walks alongside us. Sometimes that shadow grew longer and larger before the light of her flame balanced it out.

The flame flickers as it nears the end of the wick. Smoke wisps curl, dancing as they rise into the air. A pungent yet sweet aroma fills the lungs as the perfume dissipates. The curling twisting wisps continue their dance, swaying, weaving, up, up and around. Each tendril alive in its own time, its own space, dancing with the other fleeting smoke-partners. Intertwined, separated, woven yet independent, they move ever upward with the gentle flows of air and breath.

The last flicker, the wick spent. The red glow of the last ember's fire-eyes sear like a snake's parting glance before disappearing. The memory of the flame lingers, along with the scent of the dancing wisps.

Family Tree

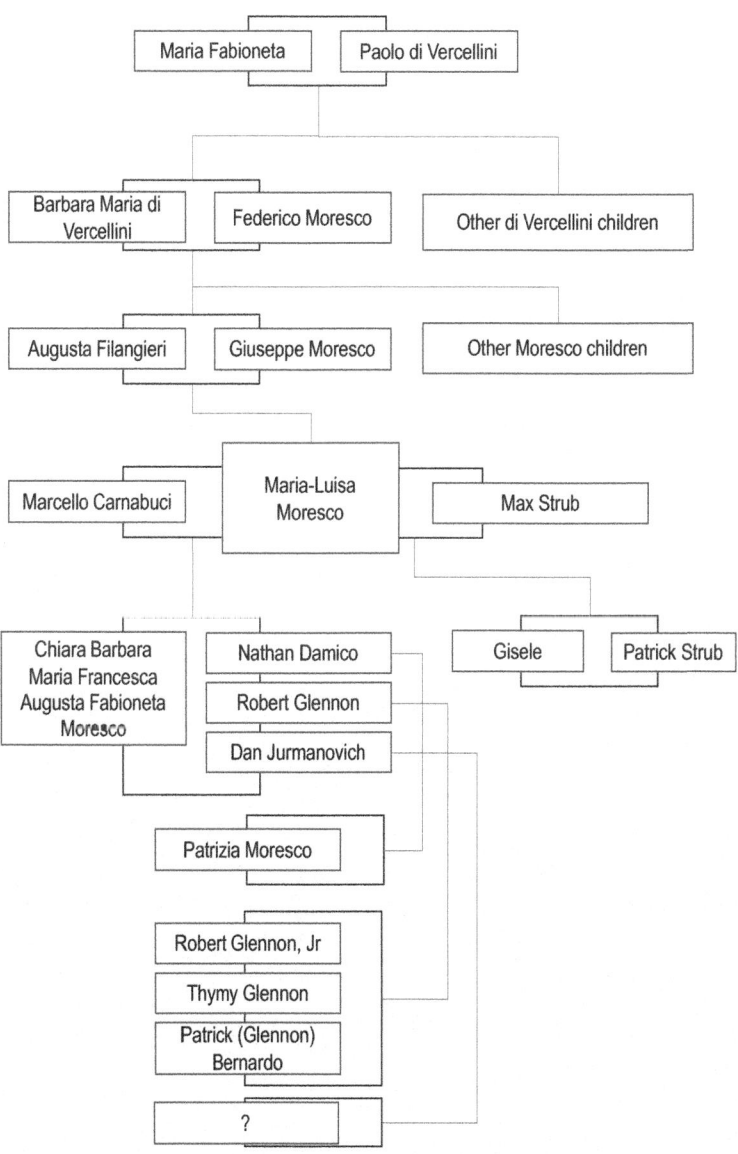

About the Author

Mark Jamilkowski was born in Connecticut and educated at Trinity College, Hartford. He has had a life-long joy in cooking, music, the arts, and games of strategy. Mark enjoys reading historical fiction, philosophy, literature, and poetry. He resides in New York City.

Special Thanks to

The Road to Moresco would not have been possible if not for the tireless dedication and editorial assistance of Cynthia Stone, whose chance meeting at a book festival in Austin, Texas, became the catalyst for seeing this through to completion.

I have deep gratitude to all those who continued to support this effort, often in moments of doubt, and pushed me even when I disagreed with them, especially Carla, Ann, Joann, Mark, Kasia, and Michelle. And of course, a special thanks to Sandra.

Bibliography

CHAPTER 1

Giovan Giuseppe Mellusi, "Dalla Lettera della Madonna alla Madonna della Lettera," Archivio storico messinese 93 (2012): 237–61.

Giuseppe Lipari, "La Madonna della Lettera nella cultura messinese," in Arte, storia e tradizione nella devozione alla Madonna, ed. Giovanni Molonia (Messina: Tipografia Spignolo, 1995), 69–79.

Giuliano, A., & Scarpari, M. (2018). The Letter of the Madonna to the People of Messina in Chinese by the Jesuit Metello Saccano: An Unknown Seventeenth-Century Manuscript, Journal of Jesuit Studies, 5(4), 631-641. doi: https://doi.org/10.1163/22141332-00504008

Britannica, The Editors of Encyclopaedia. "Messina earthquake and tsunami of 1908". Encyclopedia Britannica, 21 Dec. 2021, https://www.britannica.com/event/Messina-earthquake-and-tsunami-of-1908. Accessed 22 January 2022.

WeirdItaly, "Facts & History of the 1908 Messina Earthquake and Tsunami, 25 images". June 1, 2014. https://weirditaly.com/2014/06/01/25-1908-messina-earthquake-and-tsunami-images/. Accessed 22 January 2022.

John Julius Norwich, Sicily, An Island at The Crossroads of History, Random House, 2015, ISBN 978-0-8129-9517-6.

Lombardi Cultural Heritage, "National Opera Balilla – ONB". Domenico Quartieri and Saverio Almini, 2006. http://www.lombardiabeniculturali.it/archivi/ profili-istituzionale/MIDL000246/. Accessed 14 January 2022.

Vespa: Pensieri di qua e di la. "The National Balilla Opera". March 12, 2019. https://sites.bc.edu/ vespa/2019/03/12/lopera-nazionale-balilla-2/ . Accessed 14 January 2022.

Cox, P. W. L. "Opera Nazionale Balilla: An Aspect of Italian Education." Junior-Senior High School Clearing House, vol. 9, no. 5, 1935, pp. 267–70, http://www.jstor. org/stable/30176386. Accessed 23 Jan. 2022.

Simon Levis Sullam, Giuseppe Mazzini and the Origins of Fascism, Palgrave MacMillan, 2015, ISBN 978-1-137-51458-5.

Lucy Hughes-Hallett, Gabriele d'Annunzio, Poet, Seducer, and Preacher of War, First Anchor, 2014. ISBN: 978-0-307-27655-1

Margherita Grassini Sarfatti (Brian Sullivan), My Fault – Mussolini as I Knew Him, Enigma Books, 2014. ISBN: 978-1-936274-39-0

CHAPTER 2

Cardoza, A. (1998). The making of the Piedmontese nobility: 1600–1848. In Aristocrats in Bourgeois Italy: The Piedmontese Nobility, 1861–1930 (Cambridge Studies in Italian History and Culture, pp. 13-54). Cambridge: Cambridge University Press. doi:10.1017/ CBO9780511585227.002

la Biblioteca del Conservatorio di Torino,

"Biblioteca". https://www.conservatoriotorino.eu/biblioteca/ . Accessed 3 Feb 2022.

Turin Italy Guide, "Why We Love Piedmont". http://www.turinitalyguide.com/piedmont/. Accessed 5 Feb 2022.

Wikipedia, "Marche". https://en.wikipedia.org/wiki/Marche. Accessed 12 Feb 2022.

R.J.B Bosworth, Italian Venice – A History, First Anchor, 2014. ISBN: 978-0-307-27655-1

Conservatorio Santa Cecelia. "La Biblioteca". https://www.conservatoriosantacecilia.it/il-conservatorio/la-biblioteca-2/. Accessed 5 Feb 2022.

Bach Cantatas, "Alfredo Casella (Composer, Arranger)". https://www.bach-cantatas.com/Lib/Casella-Alfredo.htm Accessed 12 Feb 2022.

Sachs, Harvey (1995). Rubinstein: A Life. Grove Press. ISBN 978-0-8021-1579-9

Wikipedia, "Fritz Kreisler". https://en.wikipedia.org/wiki/Fritz_Kreisler Various. Accessed 12 Feb 2022.

Wikipedia, "Alfred Cortot". Various. https://en.wikipedia.org/wiki/Alfred_Cortot Accessed 12 Feb 2022.

Wikipedia, "Wilhelm Furtwängler". Various. https://en.wikipedia.org/wiki/Wilhelm_Furtw%C3%A4ngler Accessed 12 Feb 2022.

Wikipedia, "Yehudi Menuhin". Various. https://en.wikipedia.org/wiki/Yehudi_Menuhin Accessed 12 Feb 2022.

Wikipedia, "Tullio Serafin". Various. https://en.wikipedia.org/wiki/Tullio_Serafin Accessed 12 Feb 2022.

Olmstead, Andrea (2008). Roger Sessions: A Biography. New York: Routledge. ISBN 978-0-415-

97713-5. P244

Elgin Strub: Skizzen einer Künstlerfamilie in Weimar. J. E. Ronayne, London 1999, ISBN 0-9536096-0-X

CHAPTER 3

AllMusic, "Elly Ney: A Biography". Erik Eriksson. https://www.allmusic.com/artist/elly-ney-mn0002120198/biography Accessed 22 Feb 2022.

Bach Cantatas, "Elly Ney (Piano)". https://www.bach-cantatas.com/Bio/Ney-Elly.htm Accessed 12 Feb 2022.

Critical Past, "Citizens of Villach, Austria celebrate the Anschluss", https://www.criticalpast.com/video/65675041766_German-soldiers_soldiers-marching_Nazi-flags_soldiers-relaxing, Accessed 28 Aug 2022.

Catherine's Cultural Wednesdays: Empty Nest Travel, "Visiting Weimar, Germany: Best Guide to UNESCO Treasures". Catherine Boardman, 2019. https://www.culturalwednesday.co.uk/visiting-weimar-germany/ Accessed 24 Feb 2022.

StackExchange, "Who was Mathilda von Merckens and which was her castle?". User "LangLangC", 2020. https://history.stackexchange.com/questions/60731/who-was-mathilda-von-merckens-and-which-was-her-castle Accessed 3 March 2022.

Peter Muck : One hundred years of the Berlin Philharmonic Orchestra . Volume 3: The members of the orchestra, the programs, the concert tours, premieres and world premieres. Schneider, Tutzing 1982, ISBN

3-7952-0341-4, p. 278

IMDB, "All These Women". https://www.imdb.com/
title/tt0058124/ Accessed 18 Feb 2022.

Wikipedia, "Schloss Belvedere, Weimar". Various.
https://en.wikipedia.org/wiki/Schloss_Belvedere,_
Weimar   Accessed 22 Feb 2022.

Wikipedia, "Schloss Kromsdorf". Various. https://
de.wikipedia.org/wiki/Schloss_Kromsdorf Accessed 22
Feb 2022.

Weimar Germany, "Sights". https://www.weimar.de/
en/culture/sights/castles/ Accessed 3 March 2022.

Klaus-Peter Lange, Roland Dreßler: Thuringian
mansions on the Ilm. Wartburg Verlag, Jena 1991,
ISBN 3-86160-029-3

Wolfram Huschke: Zukunft Musik: Eine Geschichte
der Hochschule für Musik Franz Liszt Weimar. Böhlau,
Cologne among others 2006, ISBN 3-412-30905-2, p. 167

Wikipedia, "Munich Agreement". Various. https://
en.wikipedia.org/wiki/Munich_Agreement Accessed 4
March 2022.

Elgin Strub: Skizzen einer Künstlerfamilie in
Weimar. J. E. Ronayne, London 1999, ISBN 0-9536096-
0-X, p. 61

Heinrich Vogel: From the Diaries of Elly Ney.
Schneider, Tutzing 1979, ISBN 3-7952-0252-3, p. 54

WikiWand, "Max Strub". Various. https://www.
wikiwand.com/en/Max_Strub Accessed 5 March 2022.

Wikipedia, "Klodzko". Various. https://en.wikipedia.
org/wiki/K%C5%82odzko   Accessed 5 March 2022.

CHAPTER 4

David I. Kertzer, The Pope and Mussolini, The Secret History of Pope Pius XI and the Rise of Fascism in Europe, Random House, 2014. ISBN 978-0-8129-9346-2

John Toland, The Last 100 Days, The Tumultuous and Controversial Story of the Final Days of World War II in Europe, The Modern Library, New York, 2003. ISBN 0-8129-6859-X

Wikipedia, "Sudetes". Various. https://en.wikipedia.org/wiki/Sudetes Accessed 5 March 2022.

Wikipedia, "East Prussian offensive". Various. https://en.wikipedia.org/wiki/East_Prussian_offensive Accessed 15 January 2022.

Hitler and his generals : military conferences 1942-1945 : the first complete stenographic record of the military situation conferences, from Stalingrad to Berlin. https://www.nypl.org/locations/schwarzman/general-research-division, call number Room 315 (JFE 03-8004)

Friedrich Nietzsche, The Essential Friedrich Nietzsche Collection, 2011, CreateSpace, ISBN 978-1460991930

Castle Hotel Liblice, https://www.zamek-liblice.cz/en/ Accessed 5 March 2022.

Wikipedia, "Kokosínský del (nature reserve)". Various. https://cs.wikipedia.org/wiki/Koko%C5%99%C3%ADnsk%C3%BD_d%C5%AF_(p%C5%99%C3%ADrodn%C3%AD_rezervace) Accessed 5 March 2022.

Wikipedia, "Prague offensive". Various. https://en.wikipedia.org/wiki/Prague_offensive Accessed 5

March 2022.

Michael Waiblinger, Strub Quartet, Booklet, Meloclassic 4002, 2014

John Toland, The Last 100 Days, The Tumultuous and Controversial Story of the Final Days of World War II in Europe, The Modern Library, New York, 2003. ISBN 0-8129-6859-X

CHAPTER 5

John Ardagh, Germany and the Germans, An Anatomy of Society Today, Harper & Row, 1987, ISBN 0-06-015839-5

GIs and Fräuleins : the German-American encounter in 1950s West Germany (2002), Chapel Hill, Höhn, Maria, 1955-, located at NYPL Schomburg Center - Research & Reference (Sc E 02-1237)

Fanny och Alexander (Fanny and Alexander), Written and Directed by Ingmar Bergman, Distributed by Gaumont and Svenska Filminstitutet (SFI), 1982, film; Accessed 3/13/2022 on https://archive.org/details/fannyandalexander_202004

Van Magazine, "The Yellow Suitcases: An Interview with Jüri Reinvere". September, 2016. https://van-magazine.com/mag/juri-reinvere/ Accessed 5 Jan 2022.

Robert Moeller, Protecting Motherhood: Women and the Family in the Politics of Postwar West Germany (Berkeley: University of California Press, 1993). ISBN 978-0520205161

Vance, Meghan, "'The Tourist Soldier': Veterans Remember the American Occupation of Germany, 1950-1955" (2015). Electronic Theses and Dissertations, 2004-

2019. 1190. https://stars.library.ucf.edu/etd/1190

Donald A. Carter, Forging the Shield, The US Army in Europe, 1951-1962 (Government Printing Office, 2015, GPO S/N: 008-029-00585-9); Center for Military History Pub 45–3–1; ISBN: 0160927552, 9780160927553

Wilson, Peter (2009). The Thirty Years War: Europe's Tragedy. Cambridge, Cambridgeshire: Belknap Press. ISBN 978-0-674-03634-5. (New York Public Library SASB M1 - General Research - Room 315 call number JFE 09-5029)

MacDonogh, Giles (24 February 2009). After the Reich: The Brutal History of the Allied Occupation. New York City: Basic Books. ISBN 978-0-465-00338-9. (New York Public Library, SASB M1 - General Research - Room 315 call number JFE 08-1607)

Keith Lowe, Savage Continent: Europe in the Aftermath of World War II (New York: Picador, 2012), ISBN: 978-1250033567

http://memory.loc.gov/diglib/vhp/story/loc.natlib. afc2001001.19971/ Harry William Gaukel, Corporal, 727 MX, 37Third Armored Infantry Battalion, Headquarters Company, Army

http://memory.loc.gov/diglib/vhp/bib/loc.natlib. afc2001001.11584 Lawrence Hamm, Staff Sergeant, Army

https://memory.loc.gov/diglib/vhp/story/loc.natlib. afc2001001.46816/ Neil William Abbott, Specialist Five, 124th Ordnance Company, Army

https://memory.loc.gov/diglib/vhp/story/loc.natlib. afc2001001.45260/ - Ronald Bortner, Airman First Class, 7499th Support Group, AF

https://memory.loc.gov/diglib/vhp/story/loc.natlib.

afc2001001.73816/ Robert Walter Baird, Private First Class, 111th Quartermaster Battalion; 759th Military Police Battalion

https://reflectionsofcoldwar.blogspot.com/2012/06/us-army-in-europe.html "The Cold War in Germany: Decoded 1945 – 1994", June 2012. Accessed 5 Jan 2022.

Detlef Junker, ed. The United States and Germany in the Era of the Cold War, 1945-1990: A Handbook, Volume 1 (1945-1968). Cambridge: Cambridge University Press, 2004. ISBN 978-0-521-79112-0. NYPL SASB M2 - Milstein Division - Room 121 call number ICM (Germany) 05-3068 v. 1

Alexis Luko: Sonatas, Screams and Silence: Music and Sound in the Films of Ingmar Bergman. Routledge, New York among others. 2016, ISBN 978-0-415-84030-9

CHAPTER 6

John Ardagh, Germany and the Germans, An Anatomy of Society Today, Harper & Row, 1987, ISBN 0-06-015839-5

Deutsche Welle, "'68 Movement brought lasting changes to German society". Various. https://www.dw.com/en/68-movement-brought-lasting-changes-to-german-society/a-3257581 Accessed 10 March 2022

Iconic, "The Tragic Story of Maria Callas and Aristotle Onassis". April 2020. https://theiconic.land/2020/04/01/the-tragic-story-of-maria-callas-and-aristotle-onassis/ Accessed 5 March 2022

Wikipedia, "Former German nobility in the Nazi Party". Various. https://en.wikipedia.org/wiki/Former_German_nobility_in_the_Nazi_Party Accessed 15 Jan

2022

Uta Poiger, "Jazz, Rock and Rebels: Cold War Politics and American Culture in a Divided Germany", (Berkeley: University of California Press, 2000) ISBN 0-520-21139-1

Bergman, Ingmar "The Magic Lantern: An Autobiography", University of Chicago Press; New Ed edition (May 15, 2007), ISBN: 978-0226043821

CHAPTER 7

Alcohol Rehab Guide, "Alcoholism In Veterans: VA: The Relationship Between Veterans And Alcoholism". https://www.alcoholrehabguide.org/resources/alcoholism-in-veterans/ Accessed 15 March 2022.

Alcohol Rehab, "Alcoholism in Veterans: Outside the Armed Forces and Inside the Throes of Addiction". https://alcorehab.org/veterans-alcohol-abuse/ Accessed 15 March 2022.

Foundations Wellness Center, "PTSD, Alcoholism and Veterans: What Justin Baksh, LMHC, MCAP, Chief Clinical Officer, August 2021. Accessed 15 March 2022.

Connecticut History, "Vietnam Protests in Connecticut". October, 2020. https://connecticuthistory.org/vietnam-protests-in-connecticut/ Accessed 20 March 2022.

Douglas O. Linder, "Famous Trials: The Chicago Eight Conspiracy Trial: An Account". https://famous-trials.com/chicago8/1366-home Accessed 20 March 2022

The Chattanoogan, "Yale University: Spring 1970". Bart Whitman, Nov 2005. https://www.chattanoogan.com/2005/11/26/76466/Yale-University-Spring-of-1970.

aspx Accessed 21 March 2022.

New Haven Register, "1967 riots: 4 tense days that began 'evolution' of blacks". Mary O'Leary, Ed Stannard, Shahid Abdul-Karim. Aug 2017. https://www.nhregister.com/new-haven/article/1967-riots-4-tense-days-that-began-11813921.php Accessed 21 March 2022.

BlackPast, "The Martin Luther King Assassination Riots (1968)". Ayodale Braimah, Nov 2017. https://www.blackpast.org/african-american-history/martin-luther-king-assassination-riots-1968/ Accessed 22 March 2022.

Ocean Beach Rag, "50 Years Ago Today – May 1, 1970 – the Rebellion Begins". Frank Gormlie, May 2020. https://obrag.org/2020/05/50-years-ago-today-may-1-1970-the-rebellion-begins/ Accessed 22 March 2022.

Howard Zinn, Voices of a People's History of the United States (Seven Stories Press, New York, 2004) ISBN 1-58322-628-1

Made in the USA
Coppell, TX
25 August 2023

20779352R00174